The End of Up

The End of Up

GRAHAM COLES

iUniverse®

THE END OF UP

iUniverse books may be ordered through booksellers or by contacting:

iUniverse
1663 Liberty Drive
Bloomington, IN 47403
www.iuniverse.com
844-349-9409

ISBN: 978-1-5320-9212-1 (sc)
ISBN: 978-1-6632-1385-3 (hc)
ISBN: 978-1-5320-9213-8 (e)

Print information available on the last page.

iUniverse rev. date: 11/18/2020

Dedicated to my parents,
for their unwavering support in all things.

CONTENTS

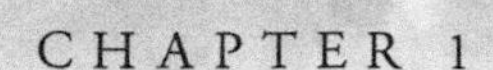

CHAPTER 1

The Arrival of Don Philips

The doctor snipped my umbilical cord, and I sent screams of triumph echoing down the stark white hallways of the hospital. Eight months later, Don's cord was cut, his howls mingling with the identical odour of disinfectant I'd smelled when I was born. Had those shrieks left hidden messages in the walls, like the cave paintings of human hands reaching from the past and into the senses of modern people?

* * *

Gnarled roots snaked across the trail, leaves fluttered in the wind, and sunlight poured through tangled branches. The path accepted our footfalls in quiet understanding; it had been host to many footsteps before. The trail wound its way around curves and corners and twists. I saw his broad back. I heard his boots connecting with the brown earth. His voice rang out: "These r-roots are gn-gnarly!"

I grunted in acknowledgment. I let out a laugh. We kept hiking, going up.

Don's powerful rugby legs were in front of me. He'd flown from Canada to experience Japan.

* * *

I'd met him at Narita Airport. He appeared around a corner, pushing a luggage cart. He had an athletic build, a goatee, close-cropped thick dark hair with flecks of grey, and blue eyes, and he emanated confidence. I stood among a crowd of other waiting people, ready to guide. He saw me and brightened.

"Hey, Gary!" he said.

"Don, buddy!" I yelled. We embraced. He started talking immediately.

"I s-sat next to this guy who talked about b-birds. Big b-birds, small birds, b-black birds, bluebirds. It sounded like a D-Dr. Seuss book!"

It was great to hear his familiar voice.

We hung out for a few days in the neon-saturated city, experiencing the packed hustle, letting words flow. Sitting together in a park one night and feeling the drizzle, we chatted about the state of the world. Gazing at the sheen of park lights and wet pavement, Don drooped his shoulders a bit and raised his eyebrows. His head swivelled my way. I saw drips form on his thick eyebrows. He inhaled slowly, deeply, expanding his chest.

"I'm a-an alcoholic," he stated.

I looked at him and nodded. Maybe it was a momentous admission for him, but we'd been close friends since we were 12 years old, and now we were well past 30. He hadn't said those words to me before.

We'd met in Grade 7, Mr. Hall's class. Don used to sit in a desk at the front of the room. One day, suddenly, he turned around, smiling wide, a pencil sticking out of each ear and each nostril. I smiled back. Mr. Hall didn't seem to notice.

Don's family had a summer home next to the summer home of George Gottfried and his family. Don, George and I were often up there shooting rocks at frogs with slingshots and beating sumac trees to death with sticks. Such destructive force lurks in boys. Sometimes that force lingers on into adulthood, unleashing destruction upon a bewildered world.

George vibrated with energy. His voice was often loud. His thick, shaggy dark hair bounced as he ran. He was a summer friend. In contrast, Don and I hung out year-round. We had heaps of good fun. Smart and athletic, he could hide his insecurities on the battlefields of North American football and traditional rugby and on the wrestling mat. I didn't join him there, choosing my battlefields in the realm of imagination. He and I built lands where swords shone and dragons flew, or where ships and tanks destroyed each other on boards. Don and I told stories; we made each other laugh. At the beginning of high school, we were unfolding game boards; by the end, we were flicking beer caps.

Over a decade later, Don and I were hiking up the mountain paths of Japan, a country that snakes along the western edge of the Pacific Ocean, its curves bordering the bulk of mainland Asia. Rectangular rice paddies cover the landscape, mountains pierce the air, and volcanoes abound. Millions of people live their lives among the convenience stores, the efficient railways and the oppressive safety.

Years earlier I had flown into Tokyo, boarded a Narita Express train and stared at futons clamped to balconies. My friend Bob Taser had lived in Tokyo for a year and had convinced me to come. I looked at high-rises stretching skyward, watery rice fields neatly arranged in flat areas, copses of bamboo leaning over roads and green life bursting forth. I existed in the busy peace. Little white trucks whizzed along, carrying the goods of economic activity. Polite young people eased me into Japan's intricacies. By the time Don arrived into this complexity, I'd been coaxing the English language from the mouths of people for years. I had assailed their ears with a barrage of grammar and rhythm and word meanings. I had been basking in the glow of being different. I was exotic.

During that time, Don had learned how to thread electrical wires through the rooms of suburban Canadian homes, encouraging light and function to blossom in human spaces. He'd worked in the cookie-cutter monotony of subdivisions and had become disenchanted. He'd gone back to school and trained as a computer programmer. He learned the languages of the machines, entered the technical world, ran marathons and stayed active.

* * *

After Don and I met at the airport, we went down the stairs to the train, through Narita Airport's massive concrete bustle and its hallways of carts and movement. On the way, he spotted a kiosk, to which his body instantly propelled him. He bought four cans of beer and tucked them away in his backpack.

"They have beers on the train," I mentioned.

Don carried his two full suitcases down a poster-adorned staircase to the platform. The floor gleamed. A guy in uniform, his white gloves gripping a broom, diligently swept.

We sat in a train that rolled us along the tracks.

"Cool b-being here?" he asked.

"Living is simple. I'm paid to be polite and punctual and to speak my language. I'm surrounded by people who exude peace," I replied.

Don's head and shoulders were framed by the train window. He stared at images of steep hills and tiny vehicles speeding down narrow roads with rice paddies dotted throughout. He looked out at the order and the busy calm of an old civilization. When the train doors slid open at Shinjuku station, he followed me out. We were met by a frenetic crush of suited men with white shirts carrying black briefcases, women clacking their sensible shoes against hard concrete floors and announcements filling our ears.

"This is intense!" he said, full of mirth.

"Welcome to Tokyo!" I spread my arms wide and accidently hit a woman in the face. "*Sumimasen!*" I bowed. She quickly bowed in acknowledgment and hurried on.

That night in a bar, Don and I engaged in catch-up conversations, his large sausage fingers gripping a glass.

"You must be jet-lagging!" I yelled above the noise.

"Not y-yet!" he shouted.

The crowd was a mix of young men and women. There was the usual low rumble of conversation and shrieks of laughter, but the words were incomprehensible.

"What's your plan?" I asked.

"I have a t-train pass," he stated. "I plan to h-head down to Kyoto!"

There was a lull in the music, so our voices returned to a normal volume. "Nice call. Check out the Sanjusangendo temple," I said.

His eyebrows lifted. "The w-what?"

"San-ju-san-gen-do. It's a cool temple full of statues," I explained. He assured me that he planned to check out all the temples.

I raised my glass, "Good luck. There are a lot of 'em."

We sat there observing. It felt familiar, similarity in a strange land.

"Give me a call when you get up to Sendai," I said.

"Most d-definitely."

* * *

Weeks later, the phone rang. Don had travelled parts of Japan by himself, had settled into the polite foreignness and had ridden the efficient trains.

"I'm in Sendai," he said. No greeting, no time wasted.

"Cool, man." I adopted the same nonchalant tone.

"Where sh-should I go?" His voice seemed tired. I directed him to the train station near my place. Later, Don's face appeared at the door.

"What a dump!" He laughed. His sarcastic wit was harsh against my ordered Japanese apartment. We shook hands and commenced with the backslapping of old friends. It was a Sunday in October, and I'd taken a week off work. I was teaching at a semiconductor corporation and had a company car.

We planned to hike up and down five mountains. Bandai-san was our first, a volcano that dominated the landscape a couple of hours' drive south of Sendai. Then we would drive to Nagano Prefecture to hike up and over Tsubakuro into the picturesque and famous Kamikochi Valley. From there we could get to the summit of Yari-gadake, one of Japan's tallest and most well-known mountains. Then we would hike back down into the valley. After a night's rest, we would go up and down Tsubakuro again and then head back to the car.

After that, I hoped we could stay a night in a *ryokan*, a Japanese inn.

Finally, we would drive to Fuji-san, the ultimate mountain hiking prize, and attain the summit as the sun rose. Then we'd drive back to Tokyo, and I'd see Don off at Narita Airport.

Our adventure was to begin the next day.

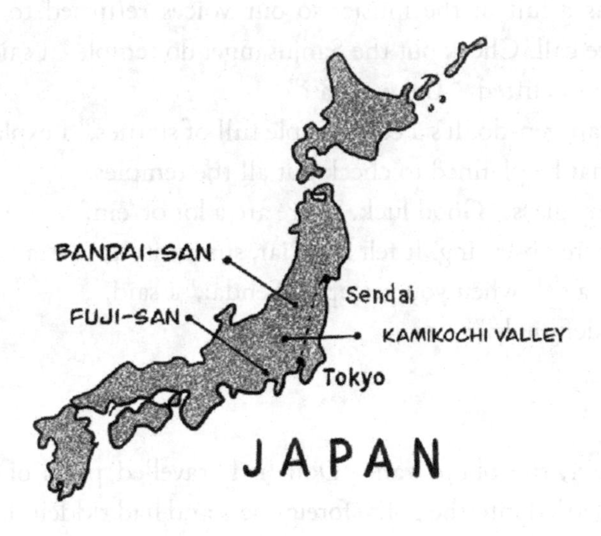

CHAPTER 2

Bandai-san

The highways in Japan weave through green rice fields and grey mountains. We negotiated the traffic lights and intersections of Sendai before arriving at the entrance to the highway. I eased the car up to a booth. A man in white gloves, a blue shirt and a black tie gave me a ticket.

"What's that?" Don asked, carefully hiding his beer.

"We're entering the Japanese highway system. When we exit, we'll show this ticket and pay for the distance we drove."

"Like a t-toll road?"

"Exactly."

We settled into a comfortable speed, the sun glinting off the windshield. Don stared straight ahead.

"So, tell me about our f-first mountain. Band-eye?" His profile filled me with a sense of ease.

Yama is Japanese for mountain. Due to characteristics of the Japanese language, sometimes *yama* is pronounced *san*. Bandai-san lords over its surroundings, towering over the farmland below.

"Bandai-san is about eighteen hundred metres high. It's a volcano. The last time it erupted was in 1888," I said. Perhaps my delivery was a bit boring.

"May I?" Don adopted an exaggerated, posh British accent and lifted another beer can.

"Certainly, sir," I replied, briefly bowing my head. "It was a major eruption." I attempted to be more engaging.

"Boom!" he yelled, ejecting a bit of spittle from his mouth.

I continued talking, trying to match his enthusiasm.

"It destroyed all the surrounding villages. Almost five hundred people dead! The explosion changed the surrounding landscape, creating two large lakes and a series of smaller ones."

"*Kaboom!*" Don inflated his chest and laughed.

I chuckled.

"It has become a tourist destination. I've been to the area a few times," I said.

"Lakes?" he asked.

My mind conjured up the regal mountain landscape of Nagano Prefecture: river valleys winding through snow-covered peaks, towns scattered along flat spaces, and car-clogged roads. Human presence blotting nature's canvas.

"I used to swim in the lakes when I lived in Nagano," I said.

"Nagano. Winter O-Olympics?" Don asked.

"Yep. We swam in those lakes."

"Who w-were you with?"

"Bob."

"Bob T-Taser?"

"Yep."

Bob and I had been swimming in lakes all our lives. Canada is blessed with an endless choice, but lakes are a rarity in Japan. In Nagano, Bob and I used to go to a lake called Kizakiko. It had an old wooden dock, presumably built for a boat.

Don stared out the passenger window at the passing hills and at the rice plants swaying next to gardens of sculpted evergreens. His eyes flitted and pulsed as the highway sped by.

"How d-did you find out about Bandai-san?"

"Early in my Sendai days, I had the luxury of exploring by car. On weekends I could pack the car with camping gear and friends and head out. After two years in Tokyo, I found Sendai to be a breath of fresh air. Sendai and its environs are less populated than Tokyo, so it's less hectic. I felt I could take deeper breaths and settle into life. I quickly tuned into that fast-paced existence of Tokyo, the excitement and rush, but Sendai has a more laid-back pace."

"Yeah, I found r-rural Japan to be way more ch-chill too."

"Where did you go?" I was curious. Had I been there?

"I w-went to Kyoto for a d-day or two, checking out the t-temples, but then I spent a f-few days up by the l-lake," he answered.

The lake? "Biwako?" I asked.

"Yep, big. I met some d-dudes camping. We sh-shared everything, food, drink, l-laughs. They were friggin' awesome."

We sped down the highway. Through the passenger window, Don stared at the undulating tile roofs of the houses, at the tidy expanse of northern Japan and at the square signs above the highway.

"Why are there English w-words on some of the s-signs?" he asked.

"It's the second *official* language of Japan." I took my hands off the steering wheel and made air quotes.

The hum of the motor reminded me of car journeys I'd taken with Don and his parents when we were young.

"Tell me m-more about hanging out n-near Bandai-san."

"A couple of friends and I headed down for a weekend of camping. One was a Brit, and the other was a Canuck from Calgary. Lake Hibara, north of Bandai, formed after the volcano blew its stack, collapsed its caldera, and slid tons of rock and earth into the river and dammed it up."

A truck passed us, white with blue writing, speeding. Its motor roared with power. The image on the side showed a bag of green tea.

"Another time, I went down by myself and hiked up Bandai-san solo. The view of the surrounding lakes was impressive. Five lakes are famous because of their colour. Owing to different mineral compositions, they all have different hues. This helps local tourism quite a bit, especially in the spring and summer."

Don looked down at his hands. "Sorry I c-couldn't come in the summer, man," he said. "F-friggin' work."

"No worries. October is a great time for hiking in Japan. Especially up mountains. The summer crowds are gone and the trails are clear. I have hiked up some popular mountains in the summer, and it was insane, a line of people on the trails all heading up. Very social, but slow. I've heard stories about Fuji-san in the summer being crazy crowded and the trails full of garbage. Hiking now, in the fall, is nice."

"Cool," Don said. We drove on in silence.

* * *

We eventually arrived at Bandai-san's parking lot. Most of the vehicles were white. I eased my grey car into an empty spot.

"We are here, my friend," I announced. We got out and stretched, grabbing our day packs and heading to the trail.

Bandai-san's path meanders up through low bushes. Don was ahead, his legs stomping out a faster rhythm than mine. The leaves were rustling and whispering. My ears became tuned to their frequency. My mind tried to convince me that it was white noise, but I was wise to my mind's ability to fool me. I felt a tug of mystery. The breeze's signals were muffled, coming from a deeper world.

George appeared in my awareness like a dream. He was erasing hit points, deep in a dungeon, concentration gripping his youthful face. Don was watching him. They were at my parents' dining room table, in my omnipotent presence. I held the dice. I held the power. I glanced at the map of the labyrinth I'd created. Don turned to me in anticipation.

My mind drifted back to the immediate, the sky, the delicacy of the leaves and the hard earth. When I rounded a corner and looked up, I saw a bench. Don was sitting on it, an open beer in his hand. He'd opened one for me too. I sat, and we looked out over a blanket of land quilted with undulating rice plants and static buildings.

"Any quotes?" he asked.

"Amit Ray," I announced as I looked at the valley below.

"What d-does he say?"

"That the universe exists in the mind like a flower exists in a seed."

Don stared at the air before adding, "Deep."

"Like the ocean," I confirmed.

We sat and sipped in silence for quite some time. A party of four made their way down the path, scuffling up dust. Gruff voices sent out greetings as they drifted past. We replied with smiles and nods. We could see little white trucks moving along the grey strips of pavement in the valley below—human activity on a supportive Earth.

Don bent over and grabbed a handful of soil. He broke it up between thumb and palm, sifted it through his fingers and then released it. He brushed his hand against his shorts as he spoke.

"When d-did Japan open up to other c-countries?" he asked.

"In eighteen fifty-three." I'd just read that fact, so it was at the ready.

"Why?" he pressed.

"Because America wanted to and had the power," I replied a bit flippantly.

"What did they d-do?"

"They sent Perry on boats."

"Perry? T-Tell me."

The wind exerted its invisible influence, deep sighs and rustles. I drifted into teaching mode.

"Commodore Matthew C. Perry sailed to Japan. The ships were larger than anything the Japanese had seen before. With their funnels belching steam, they looked like smoke-breathing dragons."

A memory sprang forth. In it, Don sat across from me when he and I were kids. The underground adventure I'd created featured a black dragon for his character, Lance, to confront. The dragon shone in the dark, its eyes flashing brilliantly, its wings stirring the air, and its nostrils sending forth grey steam from the fiery regions of the creature's bowels.

I returned to the moment, Don on the bench beside me, the large sky high above and the clear air all around. Below us, in the valley, a curving river contrasted with the straight roads and train tracks of civilization.

"I heard a story about oranges in this valley," I told him. "An orange farmer had a bunch of kids. When he got old, he divided up his land and gave it to his boys. Oranges grow better on higher ground, so he gave the uplands to his older sons. The younger ones got the land by the river because it wasn't as good for growing. Now that land is more valuable because of its proximity to the road.

"A land that had been closed for over two hundred years was about to be coaxed open. The process continues today," I said.

"Why were they c-closed?" he asked.

"The Tokugawa family gained control over Japan around sixteen hundred. They kept the country closed for over two hundred years. They only allowed the occasional Chinese or Dutch ship access for some limited trade."

He stared at me. "How do you know this?"

"I read."

"You're a n-nerd. Keep going," he said.

White clouds made their lazy way past us, unique blotches on a deep-blue canvas.

"Perry sailed across the Pacific because the Americans had had enough. They wanted to be able to fuel their boats in Japan before they plied the waters of Asia. The American president, Millard Fillmore, wanted Japan to play with the rest of the world, to the benefit of the rest of the world of course. Such were the times."

"The t-times were about to ch-change, as they always do," he commented.

"What must the Japanese people have thought? By this time, they had developed a nice way of life. Apart from the odd samurai gone nuts, they had a peaceful and cultured society. The arts were flourishing, the food was excellent, and there was enough rice for everyone. The occasional earthquake and resulting tsunami caused problems, and a volcano or two were annoying, but otherwise it was a pleasant life," I said.

"He came back, r-right?" Don asked.

"Yeah, Perry returned in 1854 with more men and more fine European wine. Capitalism infiltrated the land of sake and swords. Inflation ensued, Tokugawa fell, and the emperor was reinstated as power guy. America got their desired coal depot and trading partner. Fast-forward one and a half centuries, and Toyota RAV4s clog the US interstates and Ichiro Suzuki taps hit after hit into the outfields of American baseball stadiums. Meanwhile, Brad Pitt and Bruce Willis do commercials for big bucks on Japanese TV."

Don's elbows rested on the back of the bench. He crossed his legs at the ankles. "What h-happened at the end of World War T-Two?" he asked.

"Japan was brought to its knees by the United States," I answered.

"The bigger k-kid on the s-school playground."

"This time General MacArthur was the powerful foreigner," I went on, "the guy who entered a defeated Japan and set it off on yet another

American-influenced path. This time Sony and Toyota, Panasonic, Honda and so many other companies were the winners."

"It's cool what J-Japan has accomplished in s-sixty s-something years," Don said.

"Back before Perry, Europeans were exploring the world, when they came across this island. They were in awe of its developed culture, advanced literacy and manners. A country that had shunned the outside world for so long had created a unique and advanced civilization. But the desire for trade pushed Perry across the ocean. The winds of change and the power of steam brought him to Yokohama with barrels of wine."

"Mm … wine," Don said.

"Natives of these parts often have a hard time imagining that anyone can truly understand them. And I can see what they mean. How can we understand the centuries of cultural development that happened behind closed doors?"

"We c-can't," Don stated matter-of-factly.

"And I've been living here for years. This country is so safe, man. The culture is powerful, the food is amazing, and everyone is polite."

I stood and pretended to be giving a speech. I yelled at empty space, "Was that the world in which Matthew Perry arrived, a land of peaceful efficiency?"

"But w-what about World War Two?" Don asked. "Why did the Japanese th-think that they could triumph over a militarily superior, m-much larger, Allied-backed country l-like the United States? What was g-going on in their n-national psyche?"

"Indeed, I'm sure people who live in Hiroshima and Nagasaki would like to know," I said. I sat down.

Don added, "That's s-something else you c-can never understand."

I looked at him and had some beer.

"Perhaps delusions of grandeur clouded their judgment? I know that I deny certain things and imagine myself to be grander than I am. Multiply this by the population of a country, and voilà, crazy things happen."

When Perry arrived, was this delusional side of the culture quiet? Did the power of the sumo wrestler pale in comparison to that of the cannon?

"Perhaps technology ruled the day then as it does now," I said.

Don told me about downtown Kyoto, about all the bright lights and flashing signs. "Japan used t-technology to r-rise again," he said.

"Yeah, after the war, Japan began to make gadgets. And they make great gadgets. Japan consistently outperforms most other nations. Today it is a modern, picturesque, thriving country, as it was on the day Perry started to wedge it open."

"So, it's been open f-for less time than it was c-closed," he realized.

"Yep."

* * *

Don was standing with his pack on. I grabbed mine, and we stepped back onto the path. More up. I tried to keep pace with Don, which was difficult. Eventually, we heard our boots scrape the summit.

The top of Bandai attracted wisps of cloud. In every direction the views stretched to bumpy, mountainous horizons. The roads looked like lines on graph paper. The rectangles of the green rice fields covered the land. Don stared at the little lakes below.

"You t-told me already, b-but I forgot, why a-are they all d-different colours?"

"Different minerals," I said.

We were hanging out at the top of our first mountain. Finding some grass to sit on, with a rock to support our backs, we opened two beers.

"Why did you ch-choose to live in Sendai, man?" Don asked.

I looked at him, the invisible wind flapping his jacket. "The choice, like all choices, was made for me," I said.

"What do you m-mean, *all choices*?"

"Well, my mind guides me, but on a lot of levels I can't be sure where I'll end up. My choices are informed by the choices of those around me and the people who came before them. My mind just tricks me into thinking they're all my own decisions."

Don's face furrowed, and he rolled his eyes. "So, why d-did your mind t-trick you into settling in Sendai?"

I laughed. "I was diagnosed with MS."

Don bowed his head. "I don't get it," he said.

"Remember when I went blind in one eye in Grade 9?"

He didn't look at me as he said, "Vaguely. What d-did you do?"

"I did what others told me."

He sighed before asking, "What was that?"

I proudly stated, "Nothing. They told me to do nothing."

He looked up, his eyes narrowing. "Who are th-they?"

"The adults. I was a child."

"Poor you. Now, w-why do you live in Sendai?"

"When I went blind in my right eye—"

"Did you really g-go blind?" he interrupted.

"Well, I had to be about three feet away from the eye chart to read the big *E*."

"That's blind. But the vision c-came b-back, right?" he asked.

"Oh yeah, it came back. But for nine months, during my first year of high school, that eye was really blurry. The doctors said I had optic neuritis, that the optic nerve was inflamed. But in the spring my vision became fine again."

"Yeah, I d-do remember th-that. You couldn't be in g-gym c-class."

Instead of participating in the joy of action, I had spent those hours in a windowless study hall, in silence, surrounded by others enduring the same enforced boredom.

"And then, after living large in Tokyo for a year or so, I awoke one morning with double vision," I said. "I thought I was hung over, but it persisted for a few days, so I saw an American doctor in Tokyo. She asked if I'd ever had any problems with my eyes before. When I told her about the optic neuritis, she said, and I quote, 'Oh, you have MS,' as if she were talking about the weather."

I awaited his response to the words that had drop-kicked me into a realm of fear.

"And she rec-commended l-living in Sendai?" His eyebrows lifted.

"No! I returned to Ottawa. That's when I hung out with you a bit and got super healthy. All my symptoms gradually went away."

"Comp-pletely?" he asked.

"No, not completely. But enough that I phoned the company that I'd been working for in Tokyo to ask if I could come back."

"They s-said yes, apparently?"

"Indeed, the conversation was surreal."

"What d-do you m-mean, *surreal*?"

"Well, when I called, Ms. Goto said she would be happy to hire me back."

"Who's Ms. Goto?"

"Ms. Goto is a wonderful person. When I taught English in Tokyo, she was my main contact in the office. We occasionally went out for lunch. She had a nice figure, funky teeth. Before working in Tokyo, she had applied at Japan Airlines as a flight attendant. She said that she had been denied the job because of her teeth."

"You s-still haven't t-told me why you l-live in Sendai."

"Ms. Goto called me in Ottawa. The conversation went something like this: She said, 'Would you like to work in Sendai?' I said yes. She said, 'You would work at a semiconductor company.' I said, 'Great.' She said, 'We'll find you an apartment and pay your rent.' I said, 'Great.' She said, 'We'll pay all your utility and phone bills.' I said, 'Great.' She said, 'We'll get you a car.' I said, 'Great.' She said, 'You'll teach for thirty weeks of the year, but we'll pay you for fifty-two.' I said, 'Great.' She said, 'You'll start in January.' I said, 'Great.'"

"Gotcha. Now I t-totally understand why you l-live in Sendai," Don said.

"I know, too good to be true, right?"

"Had you b-been to Sendai before?"

"Yeah, I used to make trips up there."

"Why?"

"Crazy love."

"Gets ya every t-time," he said, grinning.

"Before I returned to Japan, and Sendai, I worked in a bookstore in Ottawa. There was a hard cover on Japan, and a young woman came in to buy it, the only person who bought that book from me. I asked her if she'd been to Japan. She said no, but added that her sister lived there. I asked where. She said, 'Sendai.' I asked the sister's name. She said, 'Katherine Jones.'"

Don sipped before saying, "I g-guess you're gonna tell me ab-about Katherine?"

"Yep. I flew from Ottawa to Toronto and then on to Tokyo, and then I took a bullet train to Sendai. I met a Mr. Sato, who ran the training programs at the semiconductor company. He had a serious face."

"Tell m-me about Katherine," he said.

"Kate," I corrected.

Don's eyes rolled.

"Mr. Sato talked a lot about Sendai. He made me feel very welcome. As we drove to the semiconductor facilities, he told me he knew someone who wanted to meet me. For fun I asked if her name was Katherine Jones. He looked at me strangely and then said, 'Yes.'"

"Small w-w-world," Don said.

"And mysterious," I added. "Anyway, Kate lives in Tokyo now. I'll give her a call when we're there in few days."

* * *

"What is M-MS anyway, man?" Don asked. "When I f-first heard you had it, I wondered if y-you were going to d-die."

He turned to face me. The rock that supported our backs was stable and strong, light grey and freckled with green lichen, big enough to support both our backs comfortably. The sky was a dome of unwavering blue.

I really wondered how to answer that question. What *is* MS?

"It's an autoimmune disease that attacks myelin," I said.

"What's m-myelin?" he asked, looking at me, alert.

"The protective covering for nerves. MS damages the nervous system, which affects the muscles. Muscles power everything, so the affliction ever so gradually removes the body's ability to move. I guess it affects all nerves and all muscles. It affects everyone differently." I trailed off. It felt like I was vomiting knowledge, just spewing random facts.

"Is there anything you c-can do?"

"Cross my fingers and have another beer," I said.

* * *

Don seemed relaxed. Had exercise helped him settle into his surroundings? He was quiet for a while, and then he punched me in the arm.

"Got any s-stories about Sendai?"

"I used to take trips in my car. One time, I remember, I was listening to Santana's latest CD as I drove."

"I l-love Santana!" he yelled. The other hikers at the summit looked at us.

"The album has the song 'Smooth' on it. I decided that when I heard that song, I would have to camp at the next available spot. One of the nice things about Japan is that you can camp just about anywhere. The Japanese, as a people, don't camp just about anywhere; they only camp at campsites. Back in Canada, we need to limit the places where you can camp because given the chance, people would throw a tent anywhere. So, as a Canadian who likes to camp, I think Japan is great, especially northern Japan, where it is less crowded than the Tokyo region. So, I was driving through the countryside when 'Smooth' started playing. Almost right away I saw a flat, grassy area next to the road with stairs leading down to a valley. I pulled over."

Don's eyes were closed. The wind gently stirred as other people strolled around.

"You camped?" he asked, eyes still closed.

"Yep. I had a small tent, and it fit nicely on the grass between my car and a hedge. After I'd set up, I headed down the stairs. They led to a children's dinosaur theme park. There was a huge brontosaurus with a roller slide that went from its head to its tail. I'd never seen anything like it. The slide portion was made up of rollers like you see at the beer store, so instead of sliding, you whizz down the rollers. It was early spring. There were still patches of snow on the ground, and I was alone in the park. I couldn't help myself. I went for a brontosaurus roll. I laughed out loud. But the rollers were wet, and my pants got soaked."

"A brontosaurus?" Don's eyebrows raised.

"Long neck, long tail."

"With r-rollers?" he asked, incredulous.

"Yep."

"The next day I drove down to the coast with my wet pants hanging over the passenger seat. I found a temple at the top of a cliff. The gardens were manicured in a pleasing way, and the parking lot was empty. So, of course, I set up camp in the temple garden."

"Between the g-graves?" he asked.

"No graves that I remember. Nice shrubbery though. The temple was no bigger than a large house. Tall trees surrounded it," I said.

Everyone at the top of the mountain was talking and laughing. There was a group of eight twittering the loudest. Don's fingers were interlaced across his chest.

"That night I got out of the tent to pee and saw a line of flashlights heading toward me. I shouted out a greeting. Six police officers walked up. We exchanged pleasantries, and they asked about the coldness of the night and if I was okay. I assured them that I was. My identification cards were in the car, so they asked me to accompany them back to my vehicle. On the walk to the car, I kept hearing them talk about *jisatsu*, which I was pretty sure meant suicide. But why would they be talking about suicide?"

"Because you were c-camping alone in a temple g-garden?" he offered.

I laughed before saying, "Well, as it turns out, when people commit suicide by jumping off a cliff, they often take off their pants first. My brontosaurus slide–soaked pants were still hanging in my car. They thought someone might be planning to end it all. I assured them I wasn't going to jump. We chatted for a while about where I was from and how I liked Japan. We laughed a lot. Then they drove off in their little cruisers, and I went back to my temple garden camping spot."

Don and I moved to a recently vacated bench. We were each drinking a can of beer. Other hikers warned us about drinking alcohol at elevation. We politely but consistently ignored them.

* * *

Don leaned forward, his elbows on his knees. He stared out at the jagged horizon, the white peaks off to the west and the squares of a cultivated landscape below. He licked his lips slowly before he spoke. "She is c-concerned but d-doesn't seem to be on a c-c-crusade."

"Who?" I asked.

"Jean."

"The woman you're seeing?" I prodded.

"She doesn't d-drink. Maybe she'll inspire me."

The land below was mottled. All the city busyness was distant.

"You need to inspire yourself," I stated.

Don took a few gulps of his beer. I watched his throat pulsate. "I'm inspired, man. We h-hiked up our first mountain!" He cracked open another beer and smiled at me. He said, "More everything!"

I looked at him and smiled back. "Good to hang with you, man. Yeah, more everything. Cheers!" We tapped cans and stared out over the expanse of space. Up had ended. George flickered in and out of my mind.

Don asked, "Got any more Sendai s-stories?"

"Lots. I've been living there for three years," I replied.

The airy breeze at the summit smelled fresh. White cumulous clouds punctuated the piercing blue of the sky. "I'd only lived in Sendai for a few days, and when I arrived, I was fit. I had been diagnosed with MS and had determined to be super healthy. This involved eating right. So, I asked the only English speaker I knew at the time, Kate, where I could buy healthy food. She directed me to a little shop that was full of that kind of stuff."

Did Don care about healthy food?

"While in the shop, I struck up a conversation with an Italian woman. She told me about a group called Talk in English, of which she was a member. I accepted her invitation to join their next meeting."

Don sipped his beer.

"The group consisted of about ten Japanese women, the Italian woman and me. There was little format, just a chat in English. They all knew enough English to carry on full conversations. The topics varied. I tried not to talk too much. They had guest speakers come once per month to give a talk in English about their countries. One young American woman talked about her part of the States. The World Trade Center had just gone down. I remember her saying, 'Thank God Gore didn't get elected!' I recall smiling and not saying anything, but thinking the opposite."

Don erupted, "P-p-priceless!"

"I did a Canada talk once, including a Gordon Lightfoot song about a Great Lake and a ship and crew that perished, 'The Wreck of the Edmund Fitzgerald,' but for most of that year I just sat and got to know some interesting, worldly women."

He looked at me and asked, "No guys?"

"None."

"You w-were a fly on the w-wall."

"I was the only North American too."

"A weird f-fly."

"Very strange life form indeed," I said.

"Within a few days of living in Sendai, I had found a wonderful network. Many fascinating and lucrative employment opportunities for an English speaker arose out of that group. After a year or so in Sendai, I ran a regular lesson at the International Center that many of the same women attended. They were the ones who got me hired. So, when I went up to Sendai after living in Canada for a while, I was hired to give a talk. I have so many good memories of Sendai. A lot of them originated through knowing the Talk in English group."

"What kind of m-mem-mories?"

"One woman ran her own ECC Junior English School. She would pay me to come for special occasions like Halloween, Christmas or Easter. I would give a little talk about the traditions of these holidays and then listen to and comment upon prepared speeches given by the kids. I would probably do five or six of these events per year. I love that lady."

Don finished a beer and opened another one. He asked, "What does ECC stand for?"

"I don't know exactly. English children communication?"

"Easy c-cash cow?" he suggested with a crooked smile.

"Another woman set me up with a group at another community centre with people who wanted a teacher once a week. They were an older group with little English ability. However, we always had fun and laughed a lot."

"Hanging out w-with older people is often f-fun." Don rested his elbows on the back of the bench. The sky behind him glowed. George appeared then disappeared over his shoulder.

"One of the women was a piano teacher, and she taught me how to play 'Imagine' by John Lennon. I taught her kids English for an hour, and she taught me piano for the same length of time. Once, when driving down the narrow lanes near her house, I put a big dent in the company car. It was pretty scraped up. A few days later, I found out the big boss of the company was coming up to Sendai from Tokyo on business. I was to take him out for sushi. Luckily, the dent and scratches were on my side of the car. I made sure he never saw them, though. I picked him up at the station, drove him to his engagements and then took him out for sushi before driving him back to the train station."

Don said, "He never s-saw the d-damage? Hilarious."

* * *

"Early on in my Sendai life I was encouraged by a couple of the women to enter a Japanese speech contest. They all helped me write it and practice it. One of the women was a judge for this contest. I came second out of fourteen contestants. I was the only one to get a giggle out of the crowd of mostly elderly people. The ladies wrote that line for me. Apparently, it was from a famous TV commercial."

"You were a h-hit!"

"The Italian woman and I also became good friends. She was married to an English guy who was a professor of English poetry at one of the universities in Sendai. They had two little girls, five and four at the time. They spoke perfect British English with their dad and me, and what I assume was perfect Italian with their mother. But when they spoke to each other, it was in Japanese. I tell this story whenever the topic of the language-learning brain worms its way into conversation. Children have the capacity to learn many languages purely and fluently, given enough input. It is also, from what I've read, what I've studied and what I believe, good for the brain."

"What else?" Don wondered.

"I study Japanese. I go to the house of an older gentleman, maybe in his sixties, and drink tea and eat rice crackers while he helps me through my various textbooks. Again, the ladies from Talk in English suggested this guy."

"C-cool," he said.

"They are. They have taken me under their wing, and they make sure that when I need something, it appears. I feel a great debt of gratitude toward them. I hope they find that my presence adds something too. Sendai is my favourite place in Japan. I love the proximity to mountains and the ocean, and the great job, but though these things are part of it for sure, I think the Talk in English women supply me with a social life that I wouldn't have otherwise. This surely adds to my high esteem for Sendai. They bring me close to the Japanese fabric of that city."

The sun blazed. People were wearing hats to shield their faces. The sky remained static. The summit was crowded, like Japan in general.

Don looked out and down. I could see trucks and cars moving along the road. The bench supported the muscles that had carried us faithfully up. My mind was now sending messages of descent, but still we sat.

"This is trés c-cool, my friend," he said. "B-but why do people wear t-towels around their necks?"

"To catch the sweat," I said.

If I had thought about it more, I might have said something about keeping up appearances or being part of the tribe.

Don breathed in loudly through his nose. "I love this," he said.

* * *

An old man stood up. The people around him twittered and started to stand as well. Flasks were returned to backpacks, and I heard the sound of rustling and stuffing. There were eight of them, four men and four women. Eventually, the group made their way back to the path, their boots scuffing the dusty earth. They all wore suspenders to hold up their khaki hiking trousers; they all had white towels around their necks; they all wore glasses; and they all had hiking sticks. Each hiking stick had a different design. One woman had a stick with a leopard skin pattern; another, with purple and yellow stripes; and yet another, shiny bells that made a Christmassy sound as she walked. Individualized conformity.

My ankles burned; they had worked hard on the ascent. My body relaxed onto the bench. Don's elbows were on his knees. Getting to the mountaintop filled me with a sense of accomplishment, like a sumo wrestler winning a bout.

"I saw the Ozekis square off the other day. I watched it on *Sumo Digest*," I said.

"Sumo w-wrestling?" Don asked.

"Yep."

"Tell me about it."

"Before I went to Japan, I thought sumo wrestling was a foreign fighting sport where fat men slammed into each other."

"Did y-you ch-change your mind?"

"I was hooked soon after arriving in Japan and watching it for a couple of days. I had never been much of a fan of fighting. Maybe I was just scared. But sumo changed my mind. Here was a fighting sport I gladly watched."

Don leaned against the back of the bench.

"The rules are simple," I said. "Knock your opponent down or out of the ring, and you win. The ring is made by a rope secured along the ground. The wrestlers face each other, and on a command from the referee, they charge. Sometimes their foreheads collide like mountain goats."

Don laughed. "*Crack!*" he yelled.

"There are no weight categories in sumo. Mainomi, a Japanese favourite, was small, maybe about one hundred kilograms. But Konnishiki was huge, weighing in at about two hundred and seventy. Mainomi, the small guy, was short, and Akebono, another dude, Hawaiian, like Konnishiki, was tall. Akebono is a Yokozuna. He's over six foot eight, man!"

"He could play b-basketball," Don said.

"He's too fat," I said. "Anyway, Mainomi beating those giants always pleased the crowd."

"Why do you like sumo w-wrestling so m-much?" he asked.

"The allure of sumo resides in the lead-up to each bout, the history of each *rikishi* and the character they bring to the ring."

"What's a r-rikishi?" he asked.

"A sumo wrestler," I answered.

"Why didn't you s-say s-so?" he said, smiling.

"When in Rome," I offered.

Don abruptly rose, grabbed his pack, and began his hike down. "C-coming?" he asked.

* * *

The clouds drifted. My hiking stirred the dust. Don was long gone. I chatted pleasantly with the hikers I encountered, the same group who were on the top of the mountain. They were on a trip from Nagoya, a big city.

The first woman I overtook had the leopard skin hiking stick. She mentioned how difficult descents were.

"Taihen desu ne!" I agreed.

Then I passed a little gentleman with a black stick. He remarked on the heat.

"Atsui desu ne!" I replied in solidarity.

The trail opened up. I could see no hikers on the path, but I could hear the tapping of multiple canes. As I rounded a long curve, I spotted the rest of the group. The first stick I joined was white with black dots. It had a woman on the end of it. She panted out a greeting.

"Konichi wa," I replied.

In front of her was a happy chap twirling a light grey and dark brown cane. He smiled at me. I smiled back.

"Saiko ne!" he said. I agreed; I was also having a glorious day.

The tapping continued. I was upon the next stick, the purple and yellow striped one, belonging to the leader of the group. He seemed sterner than the rest.

"Konichi wa!" I threw out.

He grunted his reply: "Domo."

I kicked up more dust as I passed a pink stick. The woman holding it looked up pleasantly.

"Konichi wa!"

I could see the last two up ahead, sticks tapping. They were laughing. The man's stick had bear bells on it; the constant ringing noise was designed to deter bears. I'd hiked the trails of Japan for years. I had heard the ringing many times but had seen no bears. The bells must work.

These two seemed open and curious. I told them that I had just seen a bear. They giggled. I sang 'Jingle Bells.' They bent over laughing. They wanted me to come home with them. Joking that I was on my way, I asked for their address. They shook their sticks, and the bells rang out.

I kept hiking down. The trail asserted its strength, supporting my tired legs as I worked to negotiate my descent. George entered my mind, his twinkling eyes, his long, thick hair. Then he was gone, following his own path, whatever that was.

* * *

Next to Bandai's parking lot, Don sat on a bench. I sat down next to him. "Wanna beer?" I asked in an enabling sort of way.

"Of c-course! More everything!" he stated.

We sat for a while, sipping and staring. I was lost in hazy patterns of thought. People wandered around the parking lot, opening and closing car doors, organizing things.

"What's she like?" I asked. "Your new lady?"

"We play Ultimate F-Frisbee together."

He gulped his beer, his Adam's apple bobbing. He seemed to relax a bit. The noise of car doors opening and closing continued. We stayed on the bench, resting, soaking in the end of having come down.

"What o-other volcanoes have you c-climbed in Japan?" Don asked.

"I hiked up Asama-yama once. It's a live volcano."

"When?"

"A few years ago. I saw it every day for two years. I lived to the north and worked to the south of it. Every day from the train, I could see smoke and steam billow from its depths."

"Where were you w-working?"

"At the time I was an English teacher in a little town called Komoro in the prefecture of Nagano. My working day started at one in the afternoon and ended at nine at night."

"Were you in a sc-school?" he wondered.

"Yeah, it was a conversation school. I remember the dark floors, the plush chairs and the little tables. I taught all manner of students, from little kids to the elderly, all the school ages and all types of working people looking for something to do before returning home. I rode the train every morning and every evening in those days. I always got a seat, a combination of the timing and the rural area. Later, during my Tokyo days, getting a seat on the train was a much rarer event."

"And you could see the m-mountain from the t-t-train?" Don asked.

"Yep. Zipping along the valley, I always looked up to Asama to see how much steam she was breathing. To me it was an interesting thing to see a mountain producing smoke, like an addict puffing away. From below it just looked like a mountain, not a stereotypical volcano like the mighty Fuji-san. Asama-yama was a rumbling giant, a sleepy monster in our midst. I'd been thinking about climbing her but didn't want to waste a weekend."

"You m-must have eventually w-wasted a w-weekend," he said.

"Actually, at some point, I realized I could reach the summit early in the morning and be back in time for my first class at one. I had a little white car at the time, so I could drive to the base and start hiking before the train system was awake. It was near the end of my time in Nagano, probably early spring. I'd been enraptured by views of Asama long enough, so it was time to attain the summit. I started hiking in the dark. To get up and down before noon meant I had to travel light. At the start, the ascent held views of lights from houses, streets and cars. I noticed a huge light behind me and wondered if I was seeing Tokyo to the southeast."

Cars continued to enter and leave Bandai's parking lot.

"After many steps, I turned to see if Tokyo was indeed the source of such a strong light. The realization that it was the rising sun made me chuckle. How had my mind mistaken our planet's source of heat and light as just another human creation? Had I really imagined that human power could create something as bright as the sun? I giggled to myself for the rest of the hike."

"Out of th-the d-dark, into the light," Don added.

"The wind was strong behind me, which helped with the climb. But when I reached the gaping chasm of steam and swirling smoke, I hunkered down to peer over the edge. I didn't like the wind suggesting I plummet into the depths to a quick death. I wanted to be on the other side. I had time. I gingerly picked my way around the caldera until the wind was in my face. I could peer down safely into heat coming straight from the earth. Not for the faint of heart, that view, a massive hole with lava bubbling far below and out of sight. I had thought of claiming Asama as my own, but then I realized that I was merely a guest. This was her throne. She breathed massive fire; I could only whistle in the wind."

Don sat on the bench with his elbows on his knees.

"I began my descent. Lights had winked out, leaving behind a patchwork of browns and greens. The rice fields were there, as were the trees. Rooftops lined the roadways. The trains wound their ways. No other souls were on my trail."

"Bliss," he said.

"Asama holds a special place in my hiking heart. I did a complete solo ascent of a live volcano, a view of which was a part of my journey to work every day. It didn't erupt that day. What a funky story that would have been, lava flowing beside me and fire burning the shrubbery as I made a hasty retreat. Ash raining down on me as I escaped with etched memories."

"Implanted on y-your brain," he said.

Don stood up and put his empty can in his pack. He jumped down to the parking lot surface and headed for the car. The image of him walking away reminded me of a time in high school when I'd convinced him to try a backflip off the high bar. Classmates flew gracefully through the air, and thick blue crash mats kept heads from colliding with the solid hardwood floor. Mr. Harrods, our gym teacher, kept watch over the scene, his face healthy and his arms tanned.

"It's easy," I said. Don was hesitant, but because I found it straightforward, I assumed he would too.

"Just swing and let go. Momentum will pull you through the flip. I've been doing it all morning."

Maybe a sense of competition got the best of him. He got on the high bar, he swung and he let go, but he only flipped halfway. His big body connected with the mat headfirst. His whole frame crumpled as his neck took the brunt. Mr. Harrods was on the scene quickly, sun-soaked arms checking bones and reassuring Don that he was okay. Don walked away holding his neck and giving me a pissed-off stare.

He avoided me for a few days.

That had happened more than a decade earlier. I couldn't fathom what images plagued his mind as he walked across Bandai-san's parking lot on this day. I joined him at the car. We got in, closing doors with a satisfying slam. We were on our way.

I turned left onto a minor road. The smell of our camping gear wafted through the car's interior.

"What's n-next?" he asked.

"We drive."

* * *

We passed a square building with a familiar blue and white sign indicating a Lawson's convenience store. The sign featured one of the few written Japanese characters that Don recognized.

"Booze!" he yelled, arms raised.

"Wanna stop?" I knew the answer. His hand was ready to open the car door.

"How long are we gonna be driving?" he asked.

"A few hours."

He returned to the car with six cans in a bag.

We entered the highway system. Cars, roads and signs blurred by us as we snaked through low hills and wet rice fields.

Don asked, "Why did you c-come to Japan f-for the Olympics?"

"I got a call from an American ex-lawyer dude named Craig, who'd run away to Ueda, Japan, and made quite a name for himself in those parts."

"Run away?" he asked.

"Yeah, maybe from a relationship, maybe from his parents, maybe toward adventure."

Through Don's window I could see houses with tiled roofs. He was quiet, so I kept talking.

"Craig, having taken it upon himself to learn Japanese, did an admirable job. Somehow, he had managed to get a contract with Kodak to supply drivers for the Nagano Olympics. He wondered if I wanted to be one of them. He called and asked. I decided to go. I chose adventure."

Don sipped. I drove and continued talking. "Craig lived in a drafty old Japanese place that housed us drivers. It was a busy, lucrative, exciting time at the Olympics.

"I g-guess I was w-working as an electrician," he offered.

"Probably. How was that?"

"Boring. Nagano Olympics?" He'd deflected the question about himself.

I was settled now, driving the gently curving highway with my left hand resting on my thigh.

"Kodak set themselves up in the town of Karuizawa, about an hour's drive from Nagano city and another forty or so minutes from the ski hills of Hakuba. My days were spent driving Kodak execs to different places, usually Nagano City, but sometimes Hakuba, and doing my best to interpret for them. Twelve-to-fourteen-hour days. Once the Olympics were under way, we stayed in the hotel Kodak had secured for the event."

"Big h-hotel?"

"It was big. There were conference rooms where we could meet and mingle. I started to notice that many of the Kodak employees wore vests that sported commemorative pins of different companies. They were metallic, and they depicted images of winter sports with the logos of companies displayed, for example, above a bobsled or beside a skier. These guys wore a selection of these pins that grew into a collection as the days progressed. Kodak had baskets of these pins around. I didn't think much of it."

"You sh-showed me some of th-those pins, back in Ottawa. So, you drove p-people around?" he asked.

"The driving involved taking bigwigs to different venues or taking them on errands. One guy had broken his glasses and needed to get a new pair. He was incredibly grateful when I took a side trip to the optometrist and used my basic Japanese to explain what he needed. But mostly, after dropping people off in one place or another, I was free to wander around the city, feeling the buzz of the world's attention."

From the passenger seat, Don was surveying the Asian landscape, broken by the occasional golf course and its deep green. It rained a lot in Japan at times, and that water made the areas on either side of the highway lush.

"People had set themselves up on the streets selling all kinds of Olympic memorabilia: hats, scarves, mugs, plates, trinkets, pins … pins? People were *selling* pins! More to the point, people were *buying* pins, the same type that Kodak was supplying in the hotel rooms in Karuizawa. Folks were lining up to buy pins. There was a frenzy of pin buying. When we asked the Kodak guys about the pins, they said to take as many as we wanted."

"R-really?" he asked.

"Really."

Wind harassed the car. Don folded his arms. After another sip, he asked, "So, you started s-selling p-pins?"

"Oh yeah, man! When the realization hit us drivers that these pins had a street value of anywhere from thirty to sixty bucks, we started taking some downtown with us. It was insane. It was a capitalist's dream. Get something for free and sell it for big money. Money flowed into our pockets. We were in disbelief."

"Where is the m-money now?"

"Spent, long ago. One day I made twenty seven hundred dollars in an hour."

"That's a g-great wage." Don looked me in the eye and started to laugh.

Laughing along, I said, "I ran out of pins; otherwise I would have made more. The craze lasted for days, and then the Olympics were over. So, I went to the Philippines for three weeks."

"That's w-where the m-money went," he said.

"Actually, I still had money when I got back. When I returned, I bought a used van. I drove into town, and lo and behold, three weeks after the Olympics, there was still a thriving pin market on the streets. I found out about an ex-pro tennis player who was having pins made in China and selling them in Nagano. I worked for him for three weeks, selling on the street."

"You sold pins on the s-s-street again?" Don asked.

"Yep. Then I took a trip to Bali," I said.

"Still with the m-money you m-made because of the Olympics?" Don asked.

"Yep. When I returned from Bali, now nine weeks after the Olympics, they were still selling pins on the street."

"What d-did you do?"

"I joined the tennis player and settled into a life I'd never thought I'd lead, selling trinkets on the street. I slept in my van and ate a Denny's breakfast every morning. Next to the Denny's was a *sento*, a bathhouse set up for a wash and a soak in a tub. So, for a few weeks, I parked in the parking lot, woke up, washed in the sento, ate in the Denny's and then headed downtown to sell pins on the street. Sweet. Life was kinda free in those days."

"Living ea-easy," he said

"I had no bills except gas, bathing, and Denny's. I had no plans for the future and no worries about the past. I drove to the Denny's parking lot, climbed into the back of the van, slept, woke up, washed, ate and then drove downtown again."

Don adjusted the passenger seat so he could recline a bit more.

"I have no memory of any stress. I have no memories of any regrets, just a sense of disbelief."

"That kind of th-thing rarely h-happens," he said.

"Yeah. The easy money couldn't last, and it didn't. But for a few short weeks I literally didn't have a care in the world."

The car sped along the highway. There weren't many other vehicles on the road. Hills rose out of the land in the distance. Houses were surrounded by rectangular fields, rice plants swaying.

"So, is that when you w-went to F-France?" Don asked.

"Yep, ex-pro tennis-playing man had a plan. He started on me and wore me down. He wanted to send me to France with a suitcase full of pins to get ready for the World Cup. I refused at first. I liked my life here and didn't want it to end, but the idea of a free trip to France to continue my carefree days seemed more and more like the right thing to do. I'll never know if it was. I didn't like it much. It didn't have the same rhythm. I was alone, and it seemed to me that people were harsh, unhelpful, unfriendly and impolite. I travelled around and admired the architecture, but really I didn't find much else to like. I bowed out."

We drove the highway, chatting and laughing or else silently resting in the comfort of friendship. Eventually we came to the foot of our next mountain.

CHAPTER 3

Kamikochi Valley

We pulled into the parking lot as the sun was setting. The sky was pink as I quickly set the tent up on some grass next to the trail.

"Are you ready for Main Street?" I asked.

"Main Street?"

"The route from Tsubakuro to Yari is called that because it is so busy," I explained.

"I'm ready f-for Main Street. B-bring it on."

"We are about to take a route over this range into the valley of Kamikochi," I said, pointing.

Don stared up at the mountains. The route would lead us to the summit of Tsubakuro. Don sat on the grass and began eating some sushi he'd bought at the convenience store. He offered me some. We ate, drank and chatted until stars filled the sky. He asked a lot of questions about MS.

"The diagnosis was like a punch in the stomach," I said. "I was devastated. I was only in my early thirties. It was recommended that I see a neurologist, so I did. I had an MRI, and he confirmed the diagnosis. I asked what I could do. He recommended steroids."

"Did you t-take any?" Don asked.

"No, never. I went home, sat on my futon and cried—deep rumbling sobs, body-rocking convulsions of despair and sorrow. The future seemed to have been destroyed."

"You can't think l-like that, man," he said.

"I know. The next day I pulled myself together and started talking to family and friends and reading about health. I decided to give up my job and head back to Canada. Back home, I went to neurologists and asked what I should do. One said that he wished that he could give me a pill and cure me, but he couldn't. For now, he said, I should take drugs. Another neurologist said the same thing. I asked about lifestyle changes, but they didn't seem to think that would lead to a miraculous cure."

"Bummer," Don said.

"I started to see alternative healers. They were much more positive. One laid out a specific diet and told me to drink lots of water and sign up for a yoga class. For the next few months, I gave up alcohol, caffeine, meat and dairy. I drank liters of water per day, joined a yoga class and meditated a lot. By Christmas I was fine, so I went back to Japan."

"What h-happened to c-crossing your fingers and having another b-beer?" he asked.

"That came later."

* * *

Don and I awoke in the tent at the foot of Tsubakuro. We fetched food from the car and ate breakfast as we packed up and prepared to hike. Don looked up and squinted. I locked the car. Vehicles speckled the parking lot; rays of light glinted off metal roofs; and windshields blinded my eyes if I was careless.

"That w-way, I presume?" Don followed his pointing finger.

"More up," I replied, nodding at the beckoning trail, moving my legs toward it.

"This looks w-way steeper than Bandai-s-san."

"Japan has never been glaciated, so the mountains are steep," I said.

Soon his booted legs set off, his head down, his arms swinging. His backpack bobbed. I followed it for a bit, but soon I was alone with the indifferent trees, the curvy trail and my own jagged thoughts.

"We'll go up this guy and then down the other side," I'd grunted, but the only sound was the scrape of Don's boots on the trail."

We were alone. Up had begun. Don was an athlete; this kind of activity brought out his competitive side. Tsubakuro took hours to ascend.

I settled into my breathing. I began a meditative series of steps, a process of motion, the leaves at my sides fluttering on their branches. I focused on the present, on the one-step-at-a-time endeavour of getting to the top of a mountain, on my breathing and on my leg muscles. There was only one trail, no forks to consider, no decisions to make. Just up. Every now and then a view of the valley below would appear through the trees, but mostly it was just up.

My mind began to wander. It conjured up high school days with Don and our group of friends. Eight of us had gone to Jamaica for a week in March. We were going to graduate from high school that year. Most kids went to Florida by bus, but we had flown to Jamaica.

The weekend before the trip, we all went out to a bar. We laughed and danced and revelled, immersed in youth, blind to its impermanence. I remember dim lighting with bright strobe lights periodically illuminating Don on the dance floor. Some guy challenged him to a fight for some reason. The two of them began tussling in the middle of the dance floor. Don threw the guy under the bar. The guy didn't let go of Don's shirt, and it just ripped off—completely. The bouncers took notice, and we all got kicked out.

We went to another bar, where we ordered a tray of flaming Sambucas. Don drank his shot but didn't blow out the flame first. Fire ran down either side of his mouth and onto the shirt he had borrowed from someone after his own had been ripped off. I have a clear image of Don frantically patting his shirt to put out the flames.

The flames left obvious marks on his lips and chin. He didn't come to school the week leading up to our vacation. I speculate that he was too embarrassed. He did come to Jamaica, and we all had a great time. The flaming Sambuca story was told often during late-night partying in Montego Bay.

On Tsubaruro's trail, Don was basically sober. Both physically and conversationally, he had disappeared. He powered himself up and away. We had entered a world of steps and thoughts.

I tuned in to the ambient sounds: the wind pushing through leaves, my boots stomping the path, the whistles and cackles of birds, and the rhythmic cadence of my breath. My brain pinballed thoughts. I drifted into fantasy and memory.

I went to a distant time. I was in a big American car on my way to Florida. A fourteen-year-old Don sat beside me, his mother and father in front listening to the twang of Kenny Rogers. After a day or so in the car, we eventually parked outside a motel. It had an outdoor pool and a bar. Don's parents drank gin, and after they'd had a few, we could too, with orange juice. Another family had a daughter our age. Her face carried a noticeable mark running the length of one cheek.

"What happened?" I remember enquiring. She told a simple tale of leaving the school bus and being disfigured by the mirror of a passing pickup truck.

"It should have stopped," she stated, her scar glistening in the poolside sun.

* * *

I stubbed my toe on a rock, snapping my mind back to Tsubakuro's trail. I focused on my feet and boots and the twisting roots. As I rounded a corner, I saw Don lounging on a bench.

"A-after the Olympics, you went scuba d-diving in the Philippines, right?" he enquired.

"Yep, with Bob and Rich, off the island of Palawan."

I sat down next to him.

"Have I m-met Rich?" he wondered.

"I don't think so, but he lost a toenail while diving," I said. "There's a circle road in the middle of Manila with cheap guest houses and stores lining the road. Children play there, Frosty Coke bottles stand on tables while the dust swirls. We stood out because we had money. Countless people tried to determine how to free us of some of it and line their own pockets. Many succeeded. It was easy to make friends that day. We knew they weren't real friends. We were just paying our way through Manila."

Our bench by the trail of Tsubakuro afforded a view of the valley. We saw a river, a train track, and a grey highway transporting people back and forth. To the north lay the town of Omachi; to the south, the city of Matsumoto; and directly below us, the village of Hotaka. We could see it all.

"The t-toenail?" Don asked.

My mind returned to the Philippines. "Bob, Rich and I walked and talked our way through Manila's nighttime city streets. There were bars with competent cover bands playing Queen and Pink Floyd, among others. Women came up and asked us to go downtown with them. They giggled and cooed. We smiled and laughed but continued on our way. From a distance I spied an attractive woman wearing a miniskirt and high heels, but closer inspection revealed a slim man."

"Lady m-man."

"We walked three abreast, Bob in the middle, me on the right, Rich to our left. And then Rich, poor soul, found a sewer hole and dropped three feet into the muck. There was pain involved, both physical and a mark on his bravado. Up he bounced, with a little hobble where there had been a spring in his step. We found a corner store, where we bought water. We poured some on his leg, on the slime. His toe was damaged, so talk of pain became part of our banter as we continued."

"So, he l-lost a toenail?" Don asked.

"Bob said he would, and he did later, while wearing scuba flippers during our dives."

"Ouch." Don winced.

"The next day we caught a bus to the south coast of Luzon."

"Manila is on the island of Luzon?" Don asked.

"Yep. Bob and I wanted to get our advanced diving licenses, and Rich needed to get his open water. We went to Puerta Galerta, a town thriving off of diving, and got them. We entered a haze of lazy diving days and nights of raves."

"You're a p-poet," he declared.

"After that we boarded a ferry to Palawan. We crossed a chunk of ocean. Thirty-two hours. On it we met Mike, a Swede, who had a diving business. We found a guitar on the ship, and we all played. We found a box full of ice and beer, and we all drank. We found a group of friendly folks, and we all laughed."

"Cool, man," Don chimed in.

"Palawan has natural beauty and tranquillity. Far from the bustle of the big cities like Tokyo, it has the peace of people living slow. We took a boat to Mike's hideaway dive shop. He took a pee off the stern and then took an accidental nosedive with a big splash. We had to turn around and go back."

Don swigged from his can. "Why d-did you go to P-Palawan?" he asked.

"At the tail end of World War Two, the retreating Japanese military had part of their navy fleet hidden among the islands of Palawan. Their boats were disguised as islands in the Palawan archipelago, but the US military noticed that some of the bits of jungle were moving, so they bombed them. This provided us divers with awe-inspiring underwater structures."

"Awe-inspiring un-underwater s-structures?"

"Sunken warships. The torpedoes had entered the boats and exploded. The holes looked like flowers because the force of the blasts had peeled metal out and away. We swam through the flowers in eerie silence. People had died there. Rich got stuck—a line from his tank of air snagged a chunk of metal—but we got him free."

"Crazy."

"I ran out of air, and I grabbed a buddy's line."

"You ran out of air? Isn't th-that a big no-no in the scuba world?" he asked.

"Oh yeah, big time." I replied. "We all stopped at a depth of five metres and hung out. Divers wait at this depth for the nitrogen to slowly leak out of their cells. The four of us—Bob, Rich, Simon the divemaster from New Zealand, and me—were all looking at my air gauge, watching the needle as my air ran out."

"In-insane."

"I removed my mouthpiece and drew my flat hand across my throat, an indication that my tank was empty and I could no longer breathe. Bob handed me his extra mouthpiece. I grabbed it and placed it in my mouth. I exhaled sharply into it to ensure the airway was free of water before I inhaled."

"You're nuts."

"When we surfaced, I remember the divemaster looking at me with a mixture of disbelief and admiration. I had remained calm and followed the proper procedures. My tank was empty, but I was alive."

Don was looking at me, and I was looking at him. He held out his big fist in salute. I held my skinny arm aloft and pumped the air. We settled back to our beers and viewed the valley. There was a low rumble below, the sound of civilization.

"What was Mike's place l-like?" he eventually asked.

"His dive spot was ideal, a bunch of funky rooms and a large concrete dock next to the ocean. At night we all took turns playing the one guitar and singing along. We were called the Spice Boys: Rich, Bob and me."

"Who c-called you th-the Spice Boys?"

"There were three Swedish women who ran the show. They served us drinks and food and hung around. Mike had hired them. They called us the Spice Boys. They were strong, physically and mentally, and fun. Simon was a mellow guy from New Zealand who was the divemaster for us three, completing the required foursome for diving safety."

"F-four safer than three?" Don asked.

"You need to dive with a buddy meant to look out for you," I replied. "In case you run out of air."

A bit of laughter escaped Don's lips.

"There were a few other divers of the tie-dye persuasion. Nights were long and full of good cheer. I found that I would have to go to bed earlier than the other two. Perhaps my MS, as yet unknown, was lurking. I wonder about this constantly."

"You s-seem to be h-hiking okay," he said.

"I seem to be fit at the moment," I agreed.

Birds of prey circled overhead.

"How many wrecks d-d-did you dive?" he asked.

"About five, and then we had to leave Palawan. We decided not to take a ferry but to fly to Manila instead because flying was cheap. Rich called Bob 'Lucky Dog.' Lucky Dog said that Rich would lose his toenail. Sure enough, he did. One toenail was a small price to pay for fun and adventure. Memories of Palawan are still fresh."

"I f-feel f-fresh. Let's go."

* * *

Don started up the mountain, following the trail, pounding the earth. I thought of George, our late friend. I drifted into childhood memories of abandon, of believing that once moments passed, they were gone forever, and that our laughter was all that mattered. I remained on the bench for a bit longer to let my muscles rest.

Hawks soared above, outlined against the sky, two circling examples of life. I felt the wind rustle my hair. A bee sampled a few leaves, a pollinator released to the air, free of restrictions. I closed my eyes and let my thoughts and daydreams dance with each other. I rested.

Eventually, I left the bench. My legs had regained power. I reconnected to the sound of my steps working methodically toward the top. I stayed present, listening to the steady wind and the flapping leaves.

The trail followed the ridge with trees below us to the left and right. I remained focused on the roots and rocks peppering the path. When the trees parted and views of the valley below appeared, I looked up. Don was there, on a bench, his pack beside him, his legs crossed, relaxed. He was at the summit. He barked triumphantly, "That's the hardest thing I've ever done!"

This man had run a marathon.

At the top of the ascent is a cabin. There are cabins with beer available inside at the tops of many mountains in Nagano. Once we'd had a couple, happy Don appeared. We wandered along the top of the ridge for a bit, enjoying the views of two valleys, the one we'd just come from, with roads and houses, and the one we were going to that showed little evidence of human activity, just a cabin and a bridge far below us in the Kamikochi Valley.

We met another two guys, in their sixties probably. We chatted for a bit and exchanged addresses. Those guys ended up sending me pictures. Don was wearing one of my wool sweaters.

The summit of Tsubakuro blended into the ridge. The bench had views of the valley. We sat.

* * *

"So, t-tell me ab-about your trip to Bali," Don said.

"An American guy I met, from Philadelphia, called Bali a Hindu theme park. I thought it was a happy, contented place. I wandered around it, looking at the homes blending in with the trees. I biked around rice fields, looking at neatly arranged terraces. I saw a human calm framed by lush vibrancy."

"N-nice," Don said.

"Ubud is a town in the middle of the island that is famous for carvings. There were chess sets everywhere, all different kinds of chess sets." I was speaking of a European invention in the Asian tropics. "I'm sure there were all kinds of carvings, but I only remember the chess sets," I said.

"Did you b-buy one?" he wondered.

"I didn't."

"Why not?"

"No space."

"Did you f-fly into Ubud?"

"No. I landed near a city called Denpasar. Next to the city was a beach. Deck chairs and umbrellas, bars in little huts. Some guy's passport disappeared while he was swimming. Signs everywhere told you not to leave valuables on the beach. I guess he didn't believe it could happen to him. How did he fly home? No idea."

Tropical beaches often have Western people relaxing and locals working. This one was no exception.

"I sat at a hut, drinking beer, watching tourists throw Frisbees and balls. I chatted with the woman behind the bar. She had black hair. The sea was calm."

"Then y-you went to Ubud?" he asked.

"Yep, I took a bus there and found a room. It had large white tiles on the floor. Sterile, cold looking. I awoke one morning to see a huge cockroach, black against the white tile. Without thinking, I killed it."

Don winced.

"I left its corpse on the floor and went off into town to rent a mountain bike. I cycled to a fancy hotel where a 7-Up cost seven bucks. The landscape was gorgeous as far as the eye could see, no neon, no signs, no cars. Just me pedalling."

"Was the c-cockroach c-c-carcass still there when you g-got back?"

"I returned to the big white floor to find a line of ants marching to its remains. I went out for dinner. There was a dog lying on the road, panting. I ate nasi goreng. On my return, the dog was dead."

Don shifted his body.

"My room, however, had been cleaned by the ants, and there was no evidence of the dead cockroach. The next morning, the dead dog was still there. It would take the ants much longer to dispose of that carcass. Everyone seemed to go about their daily lives around the dead dog, so I did the same."

"The dog n-never got taken away?" he asked, eyebrows raised.

"Nope."

"How w-were the l-ladies?" he asked.

"Women used to go topless in Bali. Maybe this disturbed Christian minds. The Western world imposed its values, and this cultural freedom is no more. But when a Spanish artist went there over one hundred years ago, he painted breasts to his heart's content. In Ubud there is a gallery that bears his name, and his paintings adorn the walls of what is now a museum. I went to a festival, and one old woman was bare from the waist up. No one seemed to care. She wore an ornate necklace of beads."

"How o-old?" he asked.

"Ancient, and beautiful."

* * *

The valley of Kamikochi lay below us. Don stood and crumpled his empty beer cans. I did the same. After placing them in his pack, he began making his way down the trail. With his head bowed and his arms swinging, his athletic ability and his power propelled him. But his head suddenly tilted up, and his body slowed. Then, as if entering a different space, Don hung back and hiked with me.

We made our way slowly, methodically and enjoyably down. The trail switched back among the trees. He looked up the trail and at me and asked, "You w-went tree planting, right?"

We kept hiking down as I answered, "In B.C., I went with a girlfriend. It didn't work out between us."

His head swivelled to look at me. "Too b-bad," he said.

"Before we flew out west, my girlfriend and I shopped. We went to the army surplus store and bought a pop-up dome tent and huge army sleeping bags. We also bought massive backpacks to fit them all in. We flew from Ottawa to Vancouver and then took a bus to Prince George."

"Where's Prince George?"

"Quite a few hours northeast of Vancouver, right in the middle of the province. Lots of pickup trucks."

"Lots of p-plaid shirts?" Don smirked.

"Tons," I said. I remembered the rugged feel of the place. The city had sprawled itself across flatland surrounded by distant mountains.

"After meeting up with the operation in some office in Prince George, we planted somewhere in the mountains. They had us taken out on buses to the deep backcountry. The first day we were given a shovel, which we had to buy, and were asked why we didn't have steel-toed boots with spikes. We claimed truthful ignorance and got on with the day." Talking distracted me from the ache in my legs. "They showed us the basic routine. Not much to it, really: Shove the shovel into the ground, force it forward, and then down, and then backward to create a rectangular-shaped hole. Place a little tree in, and then stamp it. Repeat. Upon those first few stampings, I understood the benefit of boots with steel toes and spikes."

"I've always th-thought tree p-planting seemed hard."

"The earth was hard!" I emphasized.

"I b-bet. What d-did they feed you?" Don asked.

"There were tents set up for cooks to make us meals, and soon I found I was eating plenty. The days consisted of waking, eating, being driven to plots of land and then planting rows and rows of trees. True piecework; we were paid per tree. The first plot gave us twelve cents. The goal was always to plant a thousand trees in a day. Experienced tree-planting lifers managed two to three thousand, sometimes more, and I was always amazed at the fluidity and efficiency of their movements. This was all new, and I found it quite tricky at first. But after a few days it had become second nature. Like many things, it took a bit for the muscle memory to set in."

"How w-was it with a girlfriend?"

"Living in a tent with a grumpy companion was troublesome for sure, but we managed. We were put on a team with other couples, two fun people from New Zealand, a duo of an Austrian guy and an Australian woman, and then us Canadians from Ontario. Our leader was a guy named Ben from northern B.C. Most of the other planters were young single men."

"Did you make lots of m-money?" Don asked.

"Not really. Enough, I suppose. Part of the allure of tree planting was the image of restoring nature after it had been ravaged by humanity. Reality, as it often does, presented a different story. The land had been decimated, stripped of all life, and then burnt for some reason. We planted in a desolate place. A few trees a forest does not make. All food was served on Styrofoam plates; all little trees were wrapped individually in plastic. We were a marauding group of dirty parasites swarming over a scorched land, leaving a few trees and a lot of waste in our wake."

"A moonscape," he said.

I was following Don down the trail, listening to his rhythmical boot scuffs. I kept lobbing words at his backpack.

"We planted in three different places over those two months. The first two places were flat, so they were all right. For the third we drove higher into the mountains and repeatedly crossed a narrow valley that contained a wide mountain stream on makeshift wooden bridges. We planted in a valley with steep sides. Trees had been taken from deep in the mountains. Here we made nineteen cents per tree because the terrain was so much harder to deal with."

I kept tossing words his way.

"Almost every tree required a clamber over rocks and debris. And as we arrived, it started to rain. Three straight days of torrential downpour. All the bridges we crossed got washed away. We were trapped. Not a bad place really: mountaintops on either side, the land hadn't been burned, and a few big trees remained. We even found a picturesque lake and went for a swim."

"Brr," he said.

"Alcohol wasn't being flown in; the daily helicopter delivery just brought trees and food. At first the lack of alcohol made people edgy, but in hindsight I think it was a good thing."

"No alc-cohol? I'd be m-more than edge-edgy," he said, a big smile on his face.

"The New Zealand guy, Grahame, and I decided to take an afternoon off to scale a peak. Of my entire trip, that afternoon was the highlight. It was the first time I'd hiked up a real mountain. The snow sparkled. It was July."

"Snow in the s-summer?"

"Yep. We made sure we had two trees, some water and a few snacks. Grahame was older than me by a few years; he seemed so much more mature. I learned a lot about mountains from that guy as we made our way to the top of an unnamed peak. We really were in the middle of nowhere. Now that I think of it, only our girlfriends knew that we were going to climb a mountain. Turns out they both thought we were going to climb a different mountain, so they would have been of little help if we didn't return."

We were approaching the valley. Our strides were getting longer.

"Just two guys in the wild. We got to the top and surveyed the wondrous world around us. Mountains as far as the eye could see. Big grins on our faces. We planted our trees and snapped pictures."

"You p-planted trees on a m-m-mountain p-peak?"

"Yep, two trees doomed to die on the weather-scoured top of a mountain."

"How d-did you get down?" he asked.

"Our descent was fast. We left huge snow bowls where we slid and slid and slid, sprays of snow hitting our giggling faces. I never saw Grahame again. He had planned to create a ski resort on the South Island of New Zealand. He might have."

"What happened to y-your g-girlfriend?" Don asked.

"Tree planting came to an end. We went to the town of Penticton. Hanging out in the middle of summer, my girlfriend, as she broke up with me, said that she hadn't wanted to go out with me in the first place. Ouch, that stung. I remember the disbelief, I remember the aching heart, and I remember the feeling of loss. I remember thinking that she could have said something sooner, before we were in an army surplus store buying a tent."

"Oh yeah, that w-would have been *appropriate*." Don punched the word with sarcastic emphasis.

* * *

As the light faded, we made our way down into the valley of Kamikochi. The cabin was close. There was the pleasant sound of the river and an expansive spray of stars. We had packed up the tent at dawn next to the Tsubakuro parking lot, and we set it up again at dusk in Kamikochi. We had climbed and descended with full packs. Tomorrow would be different.

We chose a camping spot near the slow, shallow river and away from the cabin. We unrolled the tent, unpacked the sleeping bags, inflated the Therm-a-Rests and chatted about Algonquin Park.

"What kind of tent did we have when we camped with your brother-in-law?" I asked.

"Waterproof," was all Don offered.

That night, snow-covered mountaintops surrounded us. As the beer flowed, so did the conversation.

The first time I ever went camping in Algonquin Park was with Don, his brother-in-law at the time, and his brother-in-law's friend. I don't think I'd ever laughed so much or so hard. I think we were only 15, and there was no booze involved, but it may have been the first time I'd ever smoked pot.

We talked and laughed for hours, lying on our backs and gazing at the stars. Our heads were resting on a fallen log. Suddenly, there was a big bang and the log moved. Don quickly turned on his flashlight and caught a slightly dazed raccoon in the beam. For some reason, this was uproariously funny. I guess Don means so much to me because we experienced so many rites of passage together.

The night was quiet under a clear sky—no clouds, no wind.

Our Grade 7 teacher, Mr. Hall, was a cool dude. He had a huge white beard and wore hippy shirts with flowers, and sandals if the weather permitted. He had a PhD in J. R. R. Tolkien, author of *Lord of the Rings*. He taught us *The Hobbit*. He had recorded himself reading the whole thing. He would play the tape during class, and we would read along as a group. Our minds exploded into fantasy.

"Do you still read fantasy novels?" I asked.

"Yeah, st-still a c-cool genre."

As kids, we went on to read *Lord of the Rings* and began to understand artistic possibility. The game of Dungeons and Dragons erupted out of that world. Don and I played a lot when we were 13. I created and Don played. George joined us for my biggest dungeon, 150 rooms of monster adventure. I created another writing system that they had to decode as they maneuvered through the labyrinth, collecting clues. We were three young guys expanding our minds.

George committed suicide a decade later. His daughter was about two at the time.

"Do you think about George much?" I asked. The clear river gurgled quietly. I wanted to know if Don had seen visions of George like I had.

"Not m-much" was all he said.

"Are you in touch with George's daughter?" I asked.

"Yeah," he said, staring at the river.

The gentle sound of the water was soothing. The night was black and indifferent.

* * *

"Machetes," I said.

"What?" Don's head turned to me.

"That's what the guys in the jungle had." I was remembering our high school trip to Jamaica. "You best not be heading this way, mon." I tried a Jamaican accent. Don's laughter was immediate, loud and explosive. Two of our friends had rented mopeds and headed into the hills. Having ended up in the wrong place at the right time, they were simply told that the route they had chosen was "Inappropriate at this time, mon."

Don and I were quiet for a bit, listening to the river, staring at the peaks and the stars. I thought about the spinning earth and all the rotating stars. I took a deep breath and whistled it out.

* * *

After resting, Don asked, "Brett came to Japan?"

"Yeah, he flew here with his usual genuine joy. He didn't have much money, and we wanted to climb a mountain in Nagano. No money for a train, so we had to use our thumbs."

"You hitchhiked?" he asked.

"Yep. We took a train to a highway entrance. I was living deep in the calm density of Tokyo at the time, so riding the trains was a part of life. We just had to find one that took us to a highway entrance. No issues there."

Don fished two more full cans out of our tent.

"At the entrance to the highway, we stuck out our thumbs. Within seconds a van stopped. In it we saw two women, a dog and a child. They rearranged the seating and gave us the rear section. Grandma held the dog in the front. Our bags joined us in the back—two smiley guys enjoying a ride with a family.

"Nice," Don said.

"We talked a bit and winked at the curious child. She sent glances and stares our way. The dog paid no attention to us. The women were super kind and took us up and out of Tokyo into the hills. They let us out at a highway stop full of shops and machines that sold cans of coffee. We placed in some coins and heard the *ka-chunk* of hot cans. We sipped as we wandered to the exit to bring out our thumbs again."

"How f-far did you still h-have to go?" Don asked. The sound of the Kamikochi River and the view of the stars enveloped us.

"We were about halfway to Bob's place. Immediately, a young man in a nice car with his old grandmother, we presumed, stopped and invited us to get in the back. *Zoom,* we were off again, up into the mountains and through the valleys, almost to our ultimate destination. The young man and the woman had money; an envelope full of cash. They paid us no mind as they extracted a few bills to pay the ticket guy."

"Did they t-take you all the way?"

"Nope. We still had a bit to go."

Don said, "Ever up-upward."

"There were statues of huge metallic rabbits with holes in their ears in the parking area where the guy and his grandma dropped us off. Odd, we thought. We still had to find another ride."

"Art is o-oft-ten odd."

"Out came our thumbs again, and we immediately heard honking from behind. Two young guys wanted to give us a lift. They had a small car, but there was room in the back for us and room in the trunk for our gear. In between the two guys was an ashtray contraption on a flexible metal neck. They could move it back and forth when they had a cigarette. 'Tobako suite mo ii desu ka?' they asked, wanting to know if we minded if they smoked. And of course we said, 'Dozo'—Go ahead. Turns out they weren't going our way. They just gave us a lift for something to do."

"Sounds l-like hitchhiking w-worked," Don said, his head tilted, staring at the sky, and his legs crossed.

"We arrived at our destination. Bob and Darren soon met us; they lived there. As a foursome, we challenged a peak. The next morning, we drove out in a little white van to the mountain of Chougadake. The day was sunny with a clear sky above. We started our hike."

Don lay on his back. The valley floor had disappeared into the dark; the black night sky was awash in pricks of light. I continued talking about our hike with Brett.

"The sun was out in full; the snow, white all around; our hearts, light and full of anticipation. Conversation ebbed and flowed. As we left the trees, the peaks came into view. We attacked the slopes, leaving the trail to forge our own way. What an adventure, we thought. What power we possessed. The snow was deep; the slope, steep," I said.

"Cool." he said.

"We plowed through, ever up, until we reached the peak. The views, as always, were stunning. Brett took a rock from the top. Later I would see it in his aquarium, *Chougadake* written on it in white. Brett and I returned to Tokyo in preparation for a New Year's bash; the year 2000 was a day or two away. We descended on Shinjuku, to a bar called the Rolling Stone. I remember dancing and dancing as Y2K, which had elicited such fear, faded."

"Yeah, Y2K was n-nothing!" He laughed.

"Maybe," I said quietly.

"I hitchhiked a few other times in Japan, always with full success. But that first time with Brett was the most epic, at least in my mind."

CHAPTER 4

Yari

The Kita (Northern) Alps contain many of Japan's highest mountains, many over three thousand metres. Yari is the fourth highest in Japan. A short drive north of the city of Matsumoto is the entrance to Kamikochi, a famous valley. Busloads of tourists disgorge into the parking lots at the entrance to the scenic valley, then hike along a wide path next to a river. Mountain ranges flank either side of the hike. After walking into the valley, a famous bridge with sturdy red posts and ornate decorations crosses the river. Many hike to the bridge, cross it, then hike back to the parking lot. From the bridge, on a clear day, Yari towers to the northeast. *Yari* means "spear," because of its shape.

Dawn broke sunny in the valley of Kamikochi. October was cool in the shadow of the mountains. Don watched a bee make its industrious way between small plants. The bee buzzed about. Don's darting eyes followed it.

The beer the night before might have caused the late start, or maybe it was the lazy peace of the valley, but the lack of heavy packs made the hiking fast. We left most of our gear at the campsite and headed out bright and breezy of heart, somewhat hazy of mind.

The bee was gone.

Don asked, "How m-many times have you hiked this?"

"Once with Bob. This'll be number two."

Don and I hiked together. Was he tired? Was he less competitive? He seemed more willing to talk. Maybe he had opened up to the adventure, leaving more of whatever his life was like in Ottawa behind. Had we clicked into some sort of linked vision of what was happening?

"Why is Yari so w-well known?" he asked.

"Its shape. Yari's peak is a spire of broken rocks."

While hiking, we saw this pyramid-like formation. I suddenly thought to look behind us.

"There's Fuji." I pointed.

Don stared for a bit. "Awesome," he said.

"The silhouette of Fuji is truly something," I added.

Don and I entered a trance with a laser focus on up. Our bodies were engaged in the marathon of attaining a peak.

"More up," I muttered. One step at a time.

* * *

As we ascended, the wind became stronger. We put one foot in front of the other thousands and thousands of times, knowing that at the end of the upward journey, we would be able to see what was on the other side of the mountain.

Don shivered. "I'm c-cold. This fleece isn't as w-warm as I th-thought."

I had an extra wool sweater big enough to fit him. I handed it over. We rarely looked up during the hike. We studied the ground to ensure our feet were placed in secure spots. My mind wandered all over the place, but my body mustered all in the pursuit of the summit.

The footpath wound randomly and was scattered with rocks. We slogged on in quiet determination. We found a bench and sat down. I started eating trail mix, and I offered some to Don. We saw a full autumn Kamikochi Valley, leaves turning colour, last-chance hikers making their laborious ways up or down with no roads.

Memories raced through my mind. I once experienced a full-moon party on a beach in Koh Pan Ang in the islands of Thailand. I once saw the glint of a knife in front of a guy dull with the weight of desperation on the island of Nias, just off the coast of Sumatra. I once felt the power of gravity pull me relentlessly down into the salty sea in a Jamaican bay near Negril.

Don and I talked about the differences between our Canadian culture and the Japanese culture surrounding us, of the country that revered Fuji-san, cherry blossoms, sake, noodles, fish and kimonos.

"Do you know what *kimono* means?" I asked.

"No," he replied.

"*Ki* means 'wear,' and *mono* means 'thing,' so *kimono* means 'thing you wear.'"

Don laughed. "I thought it m-meant something like 'f-fancy dress.'"

"You went to Kyoto, right? Its name means 'capital city.' Tokyo means 'eastern capital.' *Kamikaze* means 'divine wind,' and *karaoke* means 'empty orchestra.'"

Don looked at me. "Wait, w-why does *kamikaze* m-mean 'divine wind'?" he asked.

"Because at one point in the past, Genghis Kahn was going to invade Japan. He amassed hundreds of ships and planned to cross the Sea of Japan. However, a typhoon came and destroyed the fleet. It took Genghis a few years to amass such a fleet again. When he attempted to cross the ocean for a second time, a typhoon arrived again and wiped his fleet out. Japan was saved. So, *kami* means 'divine' and *kaze* means 'wind.'"

"Is that why p-pilots c-crashed their planes into t-targets during World War Two?" he asked.

"Yeah, they believed that destiny was on their side."

"Rude awakening," he said.

We resumed hiking.

* * *

Don, taking a swig of beer as he walked, asked me a question: "There is a r-runaway train, okay, so you c-can see that the train is g-g-going to kill five people. You have access to a s-switch, you know, that when f-flicked will d-divert the train and save the five p-people. However, one p-person is on the t-track to which the train will be d-diverted. So, if you f-flick the switch, you will cause the d-death of one person. If you do n-nothing, five people die."

He stopped walking and turned around to ask me, "Would you f-flick the s-switch?"

"Yes," I answered quickly.

"Okay, instead of b-being able to flick a switch, you can p-push a big person off the b-bridge on-onto the track and stop the t-train th-that way. Would you push?"

"No way!" I answered even faster.

"G-good to know," he said as he resumed hiking.

* * *

We talked about our high school days, about teachers we'd shared, about suburban North America and its drawbacks and strengths, and about the sterility of the life that formed us and the excitement of experiencing a place so immensely different.

We talked about women and how they were affecting the way we viewed the world. We took it as a given that we each wanted a partner with whom to share experiences. In short, we talked about what we talked about often: life as male humans in the environment in which we found ourselves. And we laughed and generally agreed.

Kamikochi sports snow-capped mountains and a winding river. It was nice to look down and around.

Eventually, inevitably, we reached the cabin perched near the peak. We grabbed a beer before making the last thrust to the pinnacle of the rough rock tower that makes Yari famous. Maybe twenty or so people can fit on the top. There were plenty of other colourfully jacketed folks taking in the panoramic views.

How many photographs can do justice to the sheer amazement you feel up there? Everyone seemed eager to digitally capture at least a smidgeon of that awe.

Don's competitive legs powered him up the gravelly staircase near the summit. Gusty wind grabbed at and fluttered the blades of sporadic patches of grass as wispy clouds skittered by. I methodically put one brown-booted foot in front of the other. Gravity pulled me down. Muscles pushed me up, ever up.

Don was starting to relax into the peace of existence. I had felt this the day before as we descended into this ancient valley, this piece of peace. Don's angst seemed to be diminishing. His relaxed state might have been gaining strength.

Don looked at me. We shared a history, a past that stretched back to high school and beyond. I was flooded with images of flying game consoles and flashes of anger, or sunlight-bathed forest leaves and eruptions of joy. We existed in mutual confusion.

"What d-does *gen-kee dess ka* mean?" Don asked.

"*Genki desu ka* is a standard greeting, an 'Are you well?' kind of thing. The *ka* means it's a question, like *Doko desu ka*, which means 'Where is it?'"

He looked up at the peak, at the pile of rocks. There was a couple hiking toward us.

"Konichi wa!" Don waved. The woman smiled.

The fella, making brief eye contact with us, said, "Domo." They went by, jingling their bear bells.

A bird landed on a nearby rock, Don watched it hop about the low-lying evergreens. "Bird," he said while pointing. "Remember that sw-swallow and the s-slingshot?"

My mind drifted to the past, conjuring up an image of a headless swallow floating in a lake. I remember Don's words delivered from the back of a yellow canoe, a slingshot abandoned at his feet.

"It felt no pain," I said aloud into the wind.

We scrambled to the top. Crazy wind ruffled the many multicoloured windcheaters. The wind was loud, drowning out people's voices. Don and I settled onto a couple of rocks and opened beers. Many others had open beers too. We were all congratulating ourselves. We'd spent the day hiking up to this inspiring spire of boulders.

"This is a c-cool c-country, man." Don's voice was strong against the relentless wind.

The emotional impact of the view from the top of Yari joined forces with the strong wind. Our eyes watered. Yari was part of a range of mountains that stretched to the horizons, each frosted peak sending a barrage of sparkles into the sky.

"What w-was it like w-when you first got here?" he asked, his voice a happy yell.

I did my best to answer him despite nature's noise. "Within six days of landing at Narita Airport, I was on a Chuo Express to Matsumoto, Nagano."

"Near h-here."

"Yeah, quite close. I did not speak the language, and I did not jive to the culture. I was truly, utterly, completely alone. People were all around me! Japan does not lack for people, so I wasn't alone in that sense. I was alone because the entire world around me was unknown."

I stopped talking for a bit. My throat was already tired. I took a long sip of cold beer.

Don looked out over the rice fields. He yelled in my ear, "Existing in a realm w-without preconceived n-notions of you f-frees you to be whoever you w-want to be!"

I wanted to continue, but the effort required to communicate was intense. I wanted to convey that the people around me had preconceived notions of who I was, but that I knew they didn't know me, had never met me, didn't know my history and didn't even know where I was from. Where was I from? What does that question mean, geographically, culturally, psychologically, emotionally? I am from so many different places.

Don crushed his can. I sipped from mine.

Eventually, Don rose. "I'm hungry!" he yelled.

* * *

His hunger took us off the peak and into the cabin. We tucked into some curry on rice. We ate as if we were refuelling, which, of course, we were. A guy dropped by our table. He told us that we ate a lot. I translated this for Don. He roared with laughter, expressing explosive joy.

We ordered another beer for Don.

I continued, "In Matsumoto, I needed to get on a train to Omachi. I was unable to figure out how to do this. Luckily, another foreign guy was at the station and was more than willing to help. He was going the same way. He was from France, and he travelled around Japan selling French wine. I was impressed at his language ability. He made children laugh as we trundled through the valley. The children, young, wearing school uniforms, commuted by themselves despite their young age."

"Safe," he said.

"I arrived at Omachi station and bid farewell to the wine-selling Frenchman. The school where I'd be teaching was across from the station, and when I entered, I was greeted enthusiastically by the two women who were expecting me."

"Enthusiastic g-greetings pretty c-common, eh?"

"Oh yeah. When I stepped into the school, they seemed to panic and their voices took on a high-pitched urgency. I had stepped on the carpet wearing my shoes, the first of many, many foot-wear violations. Wearing the correct foot-wear in the correct locations is a major concern. You never wear your shoes inside. I've became better at correctly donning the appropriate indoor footwear, but I've never quite mastered it."

"Doh!" Don laughed.

"I don't remember much else about that first day in the school. I'm sure I would have been offered tea, and I'm sure I would have accepted. I'm sure I would have been treated very well. I can be sure because after living in Japan for a few years, being treated well is something I can rely on. But on that day, I hadn't been in Japan a full week. I was still in awe of how pleasant it all was."

"Oh yes, a p-place full of h-h-help," he agreed.

"At the end of the school day, around nine at night, I was taken to my apartment. It was on the second floor of a two-storey building. It was narrow and had three rooms in a line. We entered the kitchen. It was cold in there. I was left alone. I didn't know how to turn on the heat, so I climbed into my subzero sleeping bag, thinking that I really should have asked how the heater worked."

"No heat?" he asked, looking incredulous.

"Nope, I was cold. The following weeks were intensely lonely. I had no one to chat with. Days passed. I explored the area and wandered home at night. I began to get the lay of the land and started recognizing more of the environment. I learned to navigate through the rice paddies and neighbourhoods."

His eyebrows furrowed. "No English sp-speakers?" he asked.

"None."

* * *

"One night I entered a new area. There were neon signs with pictures of young women outside almost every little building, so it was obvious what kind of area I'd entered. I had no experience with this side of life anywhere, but I felt at a complete loss in this small town. What had become overwhelming by this time was my need for human contact. One building seemed to be advertising women from the Philippines. Their English was good, I knew. I tentatively, timidly, bashfully entered."

Don didn't say anything. We were sitting at a thick wooden table. Other hikers started to file in. Perhaps the wind was too strong.

"The interior was dark. As my eyes started to adjust, I could make out a few chairs and tables, and a dimly lit bar to one side. The place was empty except for a woman cleaning glasses and another one approaching me. The second woman was wearing black leather, a sleeveless top and a miniskirt. She had lots of bushy black hair around a wise face. She spoke to me in English. I was so relieved."

"Did you g-go in?"

"I said, 'I would like to have a drink.' She explained that I had to pay to come in, and then I could drink as much as I wanted.

"'How much?' I asked.

"'Ten thousand yen,' she said. I showed her the interior of my wallet; I had only six thousand yen. I said as much to her, my wallet still open. While laughing, she looked over at the woman polishing glasses. The polisher nodded. Leather woman reached into my wallet, took all my money and then invited me in."

Don stopped eating.

"I had no idea what was going to happen, but I went in."

Don grinned at me. "I bet," he said.

"As it turns out, there are countless bars in Japan where men pay a set fee and then sit around while young women pour drinks, look cute and chat with them."

"Hostess bars?"

"Yeah. I sat for hours conversing and drinking with this fine young woman. She poured whisky, laughed at my jokes, asked questions, never looked or acted bored, talked about anything I wanted to talk about, changed the music to something I liked and gradually removed any lonely feeling that had built up over the last few days. The bar closed at four in the morning, at which point I walked home."

"Did you ever g-go there ag-again?"

"Nope."

* * *

We began our descent, our ears battered by the wind.

During our trek down, we relied on balance. Descents are, of course, faster than ascents and are generally more fun, but they're not without challenges. Thighs and knees burn from constantly fighting gravity. Ankles can turn suddenly and painfully. Conversation tends to be somewhat muted.

I looked at the white explosions of cumulus blasting the sky. My mind pinballed within my skull. I heard the scuffing of my boots and the swish of the wind.

The last few hundred metres, on tired legs, were by the river. The sound of gurgling water accompanied the sound of our weary footfalls. The famous bridge came into sight, and the campsite was just beyond.

Don and I stocked up on beers and food. Returning the camping area, we sat and watched the sun disappear behind the mountains. We recounted the highlights of the day.

There is a photo of Don wearing my sweater among a slope of rocks. He is looking up, outside the frame of the shot. I had taken that photo from above during our ascent. He was looking up at the peak of Yari. What was running through his mind?

I thought of high school hallways mopped clean of the day's grime, the dirt from shoes removed. I thought of Don approaching, his body alive with Friday delight.

The stream bubbled, the path lay calm, and mountains surrounded us. The Kamikochi valley provided a quiet strength. Our bones rested.

We stared at the blackened peaks blocking the light, blocking the sun. Night was approaching. Our Adam's apples were pulsing. Cans were being crushed.

"I r-read about this lady who t-took up track and f-field at the age of seventy-s-seven. At the age of ninety, she p-pulled off twenty w-world records." Don was almost laughing, enjoying the moment. He enunciated all the numbers, punching them with volume.

"Fit woman," I said. Don seemed animated.

"All g-golds were p-powered by her mind. She p-plans to st-still be competing at age one hundred."

Sounded inspiring. As the signs of age appear on our physical selves, our minds can hasten our decline by giving up.

I felt my legs. My knees were sore from the descent.

Don continued, "Olga enc-courages using the brain. She does Sudoku p-puzzles. She is l-learning a new language and learning to p-play the piano. She t-takes advantage of the p-p-plasticity of the brain."

I tried to read the Japanese writing on the can I was holding, thinking that new neural networks can be created when one is deep into old age.

Japanese kanji are fascinating, I thought, puzzles of immense opportunity for brain plasticity expansion.

Don said, "Olga l-learns from her m-mistakes, taking careful n-note of what went wr-wr-wrong and trying not to do it ag-gain. If th-things go right, sh-she notes that t-too, and actively tries to r-repeat the action."

The stars began to appear. We lay on our backs and continued talking. Remembering my trip to Australia, I said, "The stars in Australia are all different. The night sky down there is amazing."

CHAPTER 5

Tsubakuro

Yari was vanquished—box checked. Don and I lingered in the tent. Our hike on Day 4 was to be up and over Tsubakuro and back to the car.

This hike was a backtrack, a retracing of our steps in a place where so many had stepped before. Don was slower now. We hiked up Tsubakuro together.

"You l-lived in England, right?" he asked.

"Yeah, at my mum's parents' place. They retired to a coastal village. I spent my summers there. And I lived there for a year when I was eight. Went to a village school."

"Just as a k-kid?"

"Once as an adult, I worked in a pub there. The pub's name was the Golden Lion Tap. It was in Barnstaple, a small, rural city in England with a pretty homogeneous cultural background. Our family friends owned the Golden Lion Tap. I worked behind the bar that summer and lived above the pub in a little apartment. I was experimenting with life."

"I r-remember that," he said. "The summer after high sc-school?"

"Yep."

"I was p-partying and g-getting ready to fail uni-university."

We were quiet for a bit. The sound of our boots connecting with the earth and the gusty wind filled the space. Views of the Kamikochi Valley extended as we ascended. The peak of Yari appeared on the opposite ridge, its spire of rocks dark against a light sky.

My mind wandered to Don as the boy I had watched turn into a man. I remembered that scene in a bar the week before we went to Jamaica, his shirt ripped off in a fight. Later, I saw a vision of the flaming Sambuca, his big hands trying to pat out the flames on his borrowed shirt.

Our plodding continued, our legs in upward rhythm. My spirits felt lighter as time away from the pressures of civilization increased.

"Why did you w-work in that p-pub?" Don asked.

"Family friends owned it. Their kids went to school with us for that year in England, and their parents and mine became friends."

"Gotcha."

"Mr. Mitchell, the owner, was a builder by trade. He gutted the old building to create a fine interior with walls and windows and an atrium. It even had an old upright piano. The tables and chairs were of mixed origin, and each little area had a unique character."

I remembered the scattering of comfortable spaces. I kept telling the story as our legs propelled us slowly up. "One side of the main floor contained a long bar with many taps for draft beers. The other side had all the tables and chairs. That was where the customers mingled, mixed, talked and relaxed."

"This is l-like a natural StairMaster m-machine," Don mentioned as he climbed up over roots, rocks and earth.

"Mrs. Mitchell, who had a flair for decoration, made the pub a home away from home. The decorations fit the atmosphere. Nothing seemed out of place, except me of course. I felt like a strange lad in a strange land. Perhaps I didn't realize it at the time. I was too young to think much at all—just breaking out of childhood really."

"How many p-people w-worked there?"

"I don't know, maybe thirty? It was a restaurant as well as a pub. The manager had silver hair and a thick chest. He was fifty years old at the time. He was the only guy I ever heard play that piano. He and I would close the pub and then have a couple of pints. Well, he drank whisky mostly. Occasionally he would play 'Bring in the Clowns' because he thought it fit his position in life."

Don laughed.

"I wonder what he thought of me. I was just some Canadian friend of the owners' family whom he had to take care of for a couple of months one summer. We seemed to get along well enough. He lived above the pub too, with his greyhound, a timid animal that reminded me more of a little deer than a dog."

"Where was the r-restaurant?" he asked.

"Upstairs. I waited tables in there until the dinner hours were over. The chef was a Welsh guy with a droopy mustache. Quite a character. He lived somewhere in town with his wife and kids. He had tattoos all over his body, with the names of his entire family dotted around amidst dragons and anchors. I've worked in a lot of different restaurants in my time. Chefs organize a whack of staff, like the conductor of an orchestra. I'd finish off my shift working in the bar, pouring pints and mixing drinks."

Don was ahead of me. Tsubakuro's trail followed the ridge.

"Mid-week I had a couple of days off, so I would take the bus to the village of Croyde. My grandfather still lived there, by the sea. We would go out for pub lunches and attempt to have conversations. He was hard of hearing and had had a stroke, or two or three, which affected his speech. He couldn't really hear me, and I often couldn't understand him. Somehow we managed to convey a bit of meaning. Being in each other's company was the main thing."

"Your mum's d-dad?"

"Yeah, he must have been in his eighties. During these visits I tried to hang out with some of my friends. I'd lived in Croyde in the mid-seventies and still knew a couple of people. I'd been reconnecting every summer. At the time, I thrived on adventure without knowing I didn't fit in anywhere. But, from what I understand, most people feel this way, that they don't belong. Hard to put one's finger on the truth … ever."

Don stared away and said nothing, hiking up methodically. I continued rambling.

"I was an observer, watching the world around me. From behind the bar at the Tap, I poured drinks and saw people whom I'd never see again. They laughed and frowned just like anybody else. A friend of my dad's and his friend would get together and wander around from pub to pub. Conversations were full and frothy. There was lots of camaraderie."

"They were o-older?"

"Yeah, decades older.

"The weeks drifted by, and I had an interesting time. I experimented to a great degree, being free. I was young and didn't know what to do. I winged it. I tried a few things. I looked out and sometimes let others in. I was testing. And then, like all good things, it came to an end."

* * *

The summit of Tsubakuro was empty, really just a slightly higher part of a minor ridge. Don sat on a bench. His voice mingled with the wind. "Way easier th-this time," he said.

"You were slower; it's easier slow. Increased speed increases difficulty," I said.

"Duh. Wanna beer?"

"Duh."

I sat next to him. Our packs lay haphazardly near the bench.

"You w-went to Indonesia, r-right?" he asked.

"It was late December. I went to Sumatra from Japan."

"Where's Sumatra?"

"It's the northern island of Indonesia. It's dusty now, but it used to be all jungle, the last stronghold of the orangutan apes," I said. "My travelling companion Grace and I took a plane from Japan and landed in

Penang, Malaysia. There was a parade that day with floats and women all waving their hands. The air was hot and humid. Our clothes felt clammy. We found cold beer and tasty food. Our senses were exposed to a new environment. There were colours galore. Clothes and storefronts, taxis and motorbikes. No apparent order, just sights and odours, and chaos, and sound. It was a maze of life."

"Maze of l-life?" he asked.

"There were people everywhere, and when they saw tourists, they pounced. We were surrounded. The next day we took a ferry to Indonesia. The port was called Belawan."

A single man made his slow way up the trail. He wore a brimmed beige hat. We watched him as I kept talking.

"We managed to find the bus and get seats. We rode through stifled air to Medan, the ugliest city I've ever seen. I could see no redeeming qualities. Other people we met were feeling similar stress, so we found a minibus and climbed inside. On the bus were a trio of Swedes, another Canadian guy and an American dude. It would turn out that we all got along famously. We travelled through Christmas and New Year's as a team, full of laughter and friendship. Seven in all."

Don said, "The g-group of s-seven."

"Good group. The minibus took us to the port of Parapat. We stayed in a nice rooming house, no bustle, very relaxing. The next morning, boats took us across a big lake called Toba that had formed when a volcano erupted a few million years ago. And then it erupted again to punch up an island. It was a party island, full of bars and restaurants, and hotels, and shops with colourful clothes. And Bob Marley music all the time, everywhere. He was dead, but on this island his messages were constant."

Don said, "The group of seven im-mersed in a reggae vibe."

"Totally. We loved the music. A couple of the Swedes had seen Marley live, and I was jealous that I would never get to see such a man on a stage. Alas, I was born too late and in the wrong country. My musical heroes were old or dead and buried by the time I was aware of what they meant to me. But really, it's their music that lives on."

"We're still l-living," he said.

Don's eyes became cloudy. Maybe his mind was wrestling with demons, unseen enemies. I stopped talking for a bit and looked out at the land in the valley below. A quilted landscape with buildings dotted all the flat spaces. George sat beside me, staring at the same endless mystery.

The lone man attained the top of the ridge. He carried a gold-coloured walking stick. His brimmed hat hid his downcast eyes as he made his laboured way.

"Konichi wa," we called out.

He looked at us. "Domo," he said, then went back to focusing on the path. I noticed he had no bear bells.

My story of Sumatra carried on. "The seven of us went to the island of Nias on a ferry. We went to a cabin on the beach, where they caught fish and baked it for us. It had so much potential, but the toilet was disgusting, and we planned to take our leave. Our hosts did not like this one bit. They got silly with threats and knives and unbelievable looks. One young guy waved a blade in our faces and explained that he would remove our eyes with it.

"My friend Grace yelled at him, 'What are you, a child?'"

"He wanted us to pay for another night, two bucks each. We paid. We packed up and not only left the cabin but also left the island. Surely, we could find a more hospitable place to greet the New Year. And so, we did. We crossed the equator on New Year's Eve and partied in some town."

"One d-day I plan t-to c-cross the equator," Don said.

"The seven broke up then, and I continued on with my new friend farther south to another town, Padang. We splurged and stayed in a fancy hotel with a fancy bar. The next day I flew alone to the largest city in the region, Kuala Lumpur, with its towers and tall buildings. Head scarves are worn there by many women, but I also saw many walking the streets looking for men to please. I travelled to caves and stared down a monkey who tried to take my water. When I stopped it, a hiss of disdain escaped its lips, but my water remained with me."

Don and I had experienced four of five peaks. He had slowed and I had sped up. Don's arms swung freely as the knee-pounding descent pummelled us.

We reached the parking lot, where we threw our packs in the car, got in and drove. Soon we were in the parking lot of an inn.

CHAPTER 6

Inn

Gravel made a crunching sound as the car tires spun. We pulled into the inn's parking lot as daylight was fading.

"I'm hungry," I announced.

"I'm thirsty," Don said.

We grabbed our packs out of the car and opened the door to the inn. A warm glow revealed a young woman behind an old reception desk made of knotty wood with a coat of high-quality shellac. Her black hair was shiny, pulled back into a tight ponytail.

"*Irrashaimase!*" she yelled with a smile. Immediately eager to help, she was polite and energetically focused on us.

We went through the check-in procedure. Bowing was involved. Don watched. After four days of hiking and scrambling, it was time for a bit of relaxation.

I turned to Don and said, "A Japanese ryokan is cool, man, I've been to a few and always feel they are a cut above any other accommodation experience."

"What's so s-special about them?" Don seemed combative in a playful way.

"The islands of Japan are seismically active, which means that there is a lot of hot water underground. Over the centuries, the native people have made bathing into an art. It is very much a part of the culture."

"Everywhere?" he wondered aloud as he stared at the receptionist clicking her computer mouse.

"Yeah, there are hot springs everywhere, so inns are everywhere too. Different regions are famous for different minerals. In some places, the *onsens* are ultra-modern; in others, they are rustic."

"Onsens?" His left eyebrow raised.

"Hot springs," I replied. "There are outdoor tubs called *rotenburo*. There is nothing on this earth that can compare to soaking in a natural hot pool outdoors with stars in the sky and snow on the ground."

"I can think of a few things." Both eyebrows lifted mischievously above a crooked smile.

We were led up some stairs and along a hallway with doors punctuating the walls. The hallway was clean, functional. Our room had no beds, just rolled-up futons in the closets. Tatami, masterly woven mats, stretched from wall to wall. Our shoes remained in the *genkan*, the floor that stretched from the hallway into the room. The genkan provides space for separation before entering an indoor area, a clear division between outside and inside. It's where we remove shoes and settle our minds. Then, after we've stepped up into the room, we put on indoor slippers.

I showed Don how to wear the supplied yukata robe, white with blue straight-line designs. I spent some time setting up the camera and tripod. We laughed and posed for a timer shot.

Don asked, "Why is everyone s-so n-nice?"

"Culture."

Don looked down. "I've seen th-these r-reedy floors before. What are th-they?"

"Ryokan rooms usually have tatami floors. These reed mat surfaces are considered the best type of flooring in Japan. The craft of making them is handed down from artisan to artisan."

George entered the room. He'd written a play.

The Ryokan—a Play

(*Lights up on stage right. The main stage is in darkness. Gary and Don are wearing matching traditional Japanese robes while walking along a hallway. Gary is wearing slippers; Don is not.*)

Gary. Did I ever tell you about my New Year's adventure with Bob, the time we slid and then fell down a mountain? The time we felt the power of gravity grab us and show us death, and then let us go?

Don. No, man. I love Bob. He glides through life scattering fun. Will there be beers involved?

Gary. Oh yeah.

Don. I'm in. Tell me a story.

Gary, *pointing at Don's bare feet.* Hey! No slippers, my friend.

Don. Doh!

(*Don runs off stage. Gary waits. In a few seconds Don returns, running. A slipper flies off. He goes back to get it.*)

GARY. Smooth move.

DON. My feet are too big for these slippers!

(*Lights up on the entire stage. A bustling dining room. There are three tables. Table 1 and table 2 are at the rear of the stage, left and right. These each have two guests wearing the same robes as Gary and Don. Table 3 is brighter and at the front centre of the stage. Gary leads Don to table 3. Miki, Yuki and Rieko, the waitresses, can be seen hustling. Miki walks by.*)

MIKI. Irrashaimase!

(*Miki joins Yuki and Rieko at the back of the stage. They talk to each other. The audience can't hear them. They cast furtive glances at Gary and Don.*)

DON. I'm thirsty. I want a beer or two.

GARY. I'll order us a couple. (*Turning in his chair, he talks loudly to Miki, Yuki and Rieko.*) Sumimasen! Bin biru ni hon kudasai. Gurasu futatsu.

MIKI. Hai!

(*Miki leaves stage left. Gary and Don look around joyfully.*)

GARY. Look at where we are, man! In a Japanese inn in the middle of snow-peaked mountains.

(*Don laughs. Miki enters and arrives at the table with two bottles of beer.*)

MIKI. Hai. Bin biru futatsu desu.

GARY. Domo.

(*Gary grabs a bottle and pours Don a glass. He leaves his own glass empty. Gary waits for a few seconds, looking at Don, who drinks and continues to look around. Meanwhile, Miki joins Yuki and Rieko at the back of the stage. The waitresses converse but cannot be heard by the audience. They glance at Don and Gary, then they disperse, Rieko to table 1, Yuki to table 2. Miki leaves the stage to the left.*)

GARY. In Japan, you never pour your own beer.

DON. Oh yeah, right. Sorry. Sumimasen!

(*Don smiles and, with pomp and flourish, fills Gary's beer glass.*)

GARY AND DON. Kampai!

(*Gary and Don clink their full glasses. Miki enters the stage with two plates of food.*)

DON. Gary, tell me a story.

MIKI, *arriving at the table with the two plates.* Kochira otooshi desu.

GARY. Arigato.

(*Yuki and Rieko leave their respective tables and meet at the back of the stage. Miki joins Yuki and Rieko. They laugh but cannot be heard by the audience. Then they disperse, Miki to table 1, Rieko to table 2. Yuki leaves stage left.*)

GARY. We hiked up a mountain for New Year's. The wind was particularly powerful. Bob and I found that if we stood straight, the wind would propel us up the mountain at ridiculous speeds. It was exhilarating. We sailed up that mountain, dancing on the rocks.

DON. Tapping to the top.

(*Don finishes his glass of beer. Gary sips his. Gary refills Don's glass.*)

GARY. We brought in the New Year in the tent with a small flask of whisky and then went to sleep. Happy New Year!

DON. Mm … whisky.

(*Don finishes his glass of beer. Miki leaves table 1, walks by table 3, and refills Don's glass. Then Miki exits stage left. Yuki enters stage left and goes to table 1. Rieko leaves table 2 and exits stage left.*)

GARY. New Year's Day was sunny and windless. And we had little plastic sleds tied to our packs. So, while straddling our packs and hanging onto the straps, we could slide easily. We enjoyed the strange looks other hikers gave us.

DON. I wonder why they were perplexed. Two dudes sliding down a mountain. Normal!

(*Don finishes his glass of beer. Yuki leaves table 1, walks by, and refills Don's glass. Yuki exits stage left.*)

GARY. Sorry, man, I didn't notice that your glass was empty. Bob and I had come down many mountains in the Japanese Alps and tried to slide down as much as possible. However, backpacks don't slide well. This time we had little plastic sleds attached to our packs—the right equipment for mountain fun.

DON. Doesn't surprise me.

GARY. We knew the slopes well and had often lamented the lack of sleds on our other descents.

DON. Bob was grinning, I bet.

(*Don and Gary finish their glasses of beer. Yuki enters the stage and refills them, emptying the bottles. Gary turns to her.*)

GARY. Bin biru, mo futatsu kudasai.

YUKI. Hai.

(*Yuki exits stage left.*)

GARY. Soon we were sliding, and it was amazing. We picked up serious speed with snow spraying in our faces. Laughing and screaming, we careened down the ridgeline past bewildered hikers.

(*Don drinks all his beer.*)

GARY. We sped off the hiking path, having too much fun to stop. We went on and on and on and on, until we had to stop. We'd come to a very steep, almost vertical, snow-covered cliff.

DON. Look before you leap, eh?

GARY. Think before you drink.

(*Yuki comes to the table with two bottles of beer and fills their glasses. Yuki exits stage left. Miki goes to table 2.*)

DON. Cheers!

(*Don finishes his glass of beer. Gary refills it. Gary sips his. Don immediately drinks half his glass. Gary watches quietly.*)

GARY. Anyway, we had a decision to make.

DON. Leap or retreat.

GARY. It was a long way down, hundreds of metres at least. The snow route curved and went out of sight with large rocks and cliff faces on either side. We surveyed the route and weighed our options. Hiking back up was possible, but we weren't even sure if we would make it by dark.

DON. You went down, didn't you?

(*Don finishes his glass of beer. Yuki enters stage left and refills it. Then she goes to the back of the stage. Miki leaves table 2 to join Yuki. Rieko enters the stage and joins Yuki and Miki. Gary sips his beer and is quiet, watching Don.*)

GARY. We made our decision.

DON. You leapt.

GARY. Yep. Crazy, eh?

DON. You never even used to hike up mountains.

(*Don finishes his glass of beer. Rieko, walking by, refills his glass. Gary sips his beer. Rieko returns to Miki and Yuki.*)

GARY. Wow, you drink beer even faster than before. Is that even possible?

(*Gary and Don both laugh.*)

GARY. So, we put on our packs and tried a controlled slide on our butts and feet. I went first. I was young.

DON. Five years ago? You weren't much younger.

GARY. I was out of control immediately. I started cartwheeling down the mountain. Not cartwheeling actually, more like bouncing. I became a rag doll with that heavy pack attached. Airborne, I would slowly spin as if in space, and then I'd make intense contact with the ground, the air knocked from my lungs.

DON. You've definitely never told me this.

GARY. I sensed more than I saw the large rocks as I hurtled past them. I waited for the impact that would surely end my life. No stiffness, no control, no reliable vision, no sound, no thoughts, just me and gravity, me and the mountain, me and the snow, me a toy in the cradle of nature. And then I was sliding, and then I stopped. I remember being alone and alive. I remember waiting for Bob.

DON. You fell down a mountain?

(*Yuki and Miki exit stage left.*)

GARY. Yep. Gravity, man. It had all the power. I had zero control.

DON. You never used to be that insane.

GARY. I've broken out of my safety shell.

DON. Keep going. How about Bob?

GARY. Bob came sliding around the corner to stop beside me. He yelled in triumph. I yelled back. We weren't dead.

(*Don looks at the ceiling and squints his eyes. He finishes his beer.*)

DON. Death is a weird thing to think about.

(*They stare at the ceiling. Then, Don, leaning, looks at Gary. Don's elbow slips off the table, but he quickly recovers.*)

DON. More beer! More everything!

(*Gary grins at Don.*)

GARY. More everything. Good to hang with you, man. Thanks for coming to Japan! (*Gary turns, his hand raised.*) Sumimasen!

(*Rieko acknowledges Gary. The stage goes dark.*)

George led me back to the reality of Don sitting across from me in the brightly lit dining room. Dinner went on and on; the beers kept coming. Some of the other diners, who were mostly mostly older than us, visited our table for a brief chat on their way out.

I found myself telling a story: "Soon, Bob and I were celebrating being alive after our epic fall. All we had to do was trudge along the valley floor to the road and Mac-chan."

"Carrying a p-pack in d-deep sn-snow must suck," Don said.

"I figured, why carry my pack in the snow? It had a sled on it, so why not push it to speed up the process? The deep snow would slow the pack down and eventually stop it. I did this a few times. We were walking down a long valley that wound its way to the road, way out of sight. Push, walk, push, walk, until my pack didn't seem to be slowing down. It was speeding up. I gave chase and was gaining on it, when the slope became a little steeper. When I was close enough to dive, I dove. I reached and I missed. I stood up to watch my pack speed down the valley and out of sight to the left. A number of long seconds later, it reappeared, and then it disappeared to the right."

"The s-story continues! Hilarious," Don said.

"Had I lost all my camping gear?" I asked. "I certainly thought so. We trudged on, following the path of my pack. Soon we started to see patches of river below the snow. The patches became bigger the farther down the valley we hiked. Had my pack ended up in the river? Maybe. On we trudged as the sound of the river became louder and louder."

"Was your p-pack in the water?" he asked.

"I'm getting to that. The stretches of river became longer and longer as we continued down the valley. Finally, I saw my pack. It had sailed toward the river and crossed it on a snow bridge and had gotten wedged on the other side. There was open water above and below it, but the pack was high and dry. I was in awe. I'd gotten lucky again. The only problem now was how to get it."

"So how?" Don asked.

"Bob had some rope, and while tied off to him, I made my way gingerly down to the river, where I crossed the snow bridge and secured my pack.

"Slide, f-fall, secure. Any more?" he asked.

"Mac-chan was waiting patiently for us."

"Bob's car?"

"We rested on the hood for a while and rejoiced that our bodies and packs were intact. We continued our descent on four wheels. The mountains retreated behind us as the town rushed to meet us. A public hot spring completed our day. We soaked outside, in the mineral warmth of a rotenburo, surrounded by snow-covered rocks and bushes, reflecting on courage, speed, gravity and power as we sipped cold beers."

We kept bantering and laughing. Don told me about working as a computer programmer.

"Piece of c-cake," he summed up.

The next morning, we left the inn. We were in no hurry. The breakfast was delicious: grilled fish, miso soup, white rice and a selection of pickled vegetables. Perhaps Don had been in Japan long enough to shed the North American ideas about breakfasts of eggs and bacon and to settle into Japanese cuisine.

We returned to the car and crunched out of the parking lot.

"Why is th-this so great? What is it about J-Japan that I l-love so much?" Don asked.

"Me," I replied, full of narcissism.

I continued talking while he began working on the cans of beer at his feet.

"Japan stands more alone than most countries. Its history dictates a singularity of outlook. From about sixteen hundred to eighteen eighty, it tightly restricted people from coming in or going out. While European countries spread their philosophies and religions to the outer reaches of the known world, Japan turned inward and developed a civilization based on refining what it means to be Japanese. There are many things to admire about Japan and the Japanese culture. And like all other cultures, room for improvement is also evident."

"I h-haven't s-seen it," Don said.

"You don't live here."

He took in the scenery through the windshield: little cars whizzing by, blue road signs with white symbols, and poles with electrical wires.

"I've spent years working here and experiencing the Japanese culture. And I know I haven't even scratched the surface of its complexities."

We were driving through rectangular fields of rice and manicured trees in gardens, on our way to the highway that would take us to Fuji-san.

"When d-did you first come?" Don asked.

"I landed in Tokyo in March. In February, an earthquake had destroyed part of Kobe. Soon after I arrived, a cult released sarin gas in the subway, killing and injuring innocents. Japan promised to be interesting, to say the least."

"I r-remember that gas at-tack. It w-was on our news," Don commented.

"When I first came to Japan, I was travelling with Sarah, a dear friend, to meet Bob, a mutual friend. We were reconnecting in a foreign land. Tokyo was indeed foreign. We struggled to get on a train, and then we marvelled at the futons hanging from the endless sea of apartment balconies we passed. The density of the population astounded us. As we entered the central core of Tokyo, the world became a claustrophobic conglomeration of buildings, roads and humanity. Our Canadian sensibilities were assaulted and awed. Though time would show me that there was a rhyme and a reason for everything, on that first day we saw only chaos. Nothing was familiar. I had lost my bearings. I had left everything behind. I was born again."

"Give me a b-break! You were the s-same guy. The environment had ch-changed, that's all," Don said as he laughed.

"But these people can't fathom who I am," I said as I smiled back at him.

"You'd be surprised."

The car sped along in silence for a bit. Fuji moved closer.

"So, B-Bob was l-living in Tokyo?" Don asked.

"In a place called Nishiogikubo."

"What?"

"Nishiogikubo. The next day, I set off on his mountain bike and became lost almost instantly. There is no familiar grid pattern to Tokyo streets. The closely packed buildings do not allow you to see any kind of landmark."

"I got l-lost in Kyoto. Tokyo must be c-crazy," he said.

"A fellow I met used this analogy for a map of Tokyo streets: Imagine someone takes a bowl of spaghetti and dumps it on the floor and then puts traffic lights at the intersections."

Don laughed as he drank.

"Tokyo wasn't a planned city like New York. It grew organically from expanding villages, much like the cities of Europe. I found a train track and followed it back to the station I knew from the previous day's travel from the airport. I made it back fine, but there was a period where I was utterly lost. That's what true travel is, I suppose, getting lost and then figuring out how to get back."

"I love g-getting lost," Don said.

"You *are* lost, my friend. So am I. That's why we get along."

He lifted his can, saying, "Cheers."

"What I've discovered about the inhabitants of Japan is that they have an amazing homogeneity. I presume this causes the eerie harmony I feel. Also, as was explained to me once, they think of others first, then their families, and then themselves. I think of myself first, then my family, and then others. I grew up where the mantras of 'Look out for Number One' and 'Be different' were sung in the hallways. In Japan, one of the mantras is 'If a nail is sticking out, hammer it down.' This is understandable given the reticence of the Japanese to conceive that a foreigner could possibly understand the nuances of their culture. And to a significant degree, I believe this to be true."

"Surely that's true for m-many cultures," Don said.

"Of course. Anyway, in my case, I gave up trying to fit in. Now I am enjoying the privilege afforded me by just being different. By and large I am treated extremely well in Japan," I said.

The highway was freshly paved. A truck passed us slowly. I could see inside. The driver was wearing a blue jacket and a white head scarf. He was sipping from a can.

"I travel extensively and find some subtle variety, but mostly I find similarity, in a good way. Everywhere I go, the food is excellent, the service fantastic, the systems efficient, and the people eager to help."

Don looked at me. "Oh yeah, no ar-argument. I love it all," he said.

"Japan has its share of problems and issues, but I feel insulated from them. I am an observer who spends my time with other observers. We exist in a bubble, bouncing around from experience to experience and commenting to each other on what we've witnessed. We live in limbo land. That's the way I feel. I float in a fantastical place, predictable, safe, highly functional and very pleasurable. The months pass by wonderfully."

I stopped talking. Don looked ahead at the bulk of Fuji-san framed in the windscreen. We cruised in silence for a while. Watching the familiar cars and trucks travelling along with us, I felt the oddity of this situation. I was in a company car in Japan with an old friend from high school back in Ottawa, Canada. It felt strange. I thought about Don, what he might be thinking. I'd painted a rosy picture of Japan, but I knew it wasn't all good. Eventually I started talking again.

"I have a feeling that I am restricted. One of the advantages, not being able to participate, has become a thing that gnaws at my psyche. I can live in a box that has been built for me, but I can't leave. I am free to walk around my cage. I can make a living, go where I am accepted, partake in some of the entertainment, experience many of the benefits, but I am always an outsider existing on the outskirts. I am out and am expected to stay out."

"Boo hoo. Can we st-stop somewhere so I can m-make a phone c-call?"

* * *

We were passing Lake Suwa. Shallow and surrounded by low mountains, the lake is famous for boat rowing teams. We pulled into a parking lot with a view of the lake. Don made his call. He was very excited and talked for a while.

On that day, the sun shone. After his phone call, we drove on to the mighty Fuji-san. I knew there was a parking lot a good way up the mountain. We decided to drive and set up camp there.

CHAPTER 7

Fuji-san

Fuji-san lives in the psyche of everyone who lives or has lived in Japan. People the world over know its shape. Few mountains hold such a place in the minds of so many. And on a chilly day in October, Don and I were parked on one of its slopes as the sun set. By the time the sun rose again, we wanted to be at the summit. Watching the sunrise from atop Fuji is an experience longed for by millions.

The parking lot sits over two thousand metres up the slope of the iconic mountain. Climbing Fuji is a rite of passage, one that hundreds of thousands undertake every year. It is a patriotic act and an important feather in any cap.

We drove up the windy, paved road of Japan's historic mountain. Pavement on hallowed earth. The bulk of Fuji sat calmly, like the Buddha.

* * *

We were alone in a parking lot of empty spaces. We gazed up at the dark beckoning Fuji and down at villages and towns turning on their lights.

Another vehicle was making its lazy way up the curves of the road, its lights off. Don and I watched a green and white van puffing exhaust as it slowly chugged up the immense mountainside. It eventually arrived and parked in a yellow-lined spot a few metres away from ours. Don and I sat on folded chairs and observed two earthy people emerge. The German-made Westfalia camper van carried a couple of Japanese. The woman was not made up, and the man had grown impressive dreadlocks. I watched with mild curiosity.

"*Konbanwa!*" I yelled. They both looked in our direction and smiled.

The van had a peace sign. I held out my can of beer in Don's direction. "Cheers!" I said. He sent back a grinning salutation, holding his golden can aloft.

The sun had just set.

The guy with dreadlocks was wearing brown and green clothes. He had a quiet demeanour and a device. It looked like a little box, a finely crafted, sanded and shellacked wooden box. It produced perfectly formed joints. The guy slowly poured green bud into the top of the box and cranked a little handle. Rolled thought-altering sticks emerged. Don and I were mesmerized, but we acted as if this were the most normal sight in the world.

The woman watched quietly. I presumed that for her this *was* quite normal. She was wearing green and brown too. The two of them blended into an existence I believed was a distant nirvana, a place beyond judgment and our intense sense of time.

These two people, driving around Japan in their green VW camper van, were used to the way molecules of THC and CBD reacted with receptors in their brains. My mind was swimming in frenetic and wonderful thoughts. The strange parking lot scene surrounded me. I became lost in the folds of it. The stars shined down meaning; the conversation was stilted but free; and time briefly ceased its relentless progression.

The couple were from Kyushu, the southern island of Japan, and had come to climb Fuji. He exuded calm, and she wore an expression of ease. Earth tones were everywhere, on their clothes, in the interior of their vehicle. The green of the pot, and its smell, mingled well with the ambience of the van and its owners.

Here I was, hanging out in the parking lot of Fuji with my high school buddy Don, and the only other people there were a pot-smoking, VW van–driving hippy couple from hundreds of kilometres away. The mountain-climbing finale had begun in clouds of smoke. When offered some joints for the climb, I declined—too powerful for me! My man Don quickly grabbed three. More everything.

We set our alarms for 1 a.m. and retired to the tent for a bit of a rest. We figured it would take four hours to get to the top. As the sun rose at five o'clock, we wanted to get going by one. Of course, setting alarms for

1 a.m. didn't mean we would start hiking at one. Boots didn't hit the volcanic dirt of Fuji until 1:30.

Fuji-san is not an interesting hike. It has no trees and no vegetation of any kind and offers no chance of seeing an animal. And on that day, we saw no other people. The path switchbacks went straight up. It was a grind of a hike. And since we wanted to hit the sunrise, we had to move quickly.

Fuji's path was wide enough for both of us to hike side by side. I started talking right away.

"I read about this guy named Jacques Fresco. Have you heard of him?" I asked.

"Nope. Did h-he m-make a soft drink?" Don said, his pace fast.

"Why a soft drink?" I asked.

"Fresco s-sounds like a soft drink."

"Tesco is a grocery store chain in England," I countered.

"Tell m-me about Jacques," Don said.

"He believed that we must declare earth's resources as common heritage for the people of the entire world."

"Good l-luck."

"Jacques has been working on a something called the Venus project. He is based in a place called Venus, Florida. He's been designing a new human system most of his life. He is still going as he approaches a hundred years old."

We wore headlamps to illuminate the trail.

"We could use a n-new system," Don said matter-of-factly.

"The fundamental concepts are the abolition of money and a transformation to a resource-based economy. The results would be the elimination of scarcity and a freeing of the entire human population to turn their attention to whatever productive endeavour they choose to pursue. The planet would have to be considered by all to be one unit. The overall philosophy would have to be to slot ourselves back into the natural rhythms of the earth. In his vision of the world, the use of fossil fuels for energy would also be eliminated."

"So, get r-rid of m-money and oil?" Don asked.

"Yep."

"Good f-frigging l-luck."

"These are two significant eliminations. Getting rid of money and oil is awfully hard to imagine. But logically, wow, it makes so much sense. A major component of the philosophy, it seems to me, would also have to be the elimination of religion from the political systems of all people. The overriding spiritualism would have to turn to the human species as the Creator. We would need to work together to develop a world for ourselves. The planning and designing, monitoring and adjusting would have to become a species-wide focus. This, in my humble opinion, is the biggest challenge."

"That, in my h-humble opinion, is a c-crazy dream. How on earth w-would that even be possible?"

"The elimination of money, fossil fuels and organized religion requires intense and compelling education. There are millions, if not billions, who would fight to the death at the mere suggestion of eliminating organized religion. And there are plenty of powerful people who want to hang on to the money generated by the extraction of fossil fuels from our dear earth."

"So, you understand w-why Jacques is d-deluded?" Don snorted.

"I find the idea incredibly compelling, despite my being in the minority."

"It'll n-never happen," he said.

The ocean to the south was black. The lights of towns and villages revealed the contours of the Izu Peninsula.

"Jacques has drawn and designed thousands of pictures of his new world. The buildings and the transport systems look like science fiction. The societies are like *Star Trek*, sleek and trim. Leonardo da Vinci envisioned countless concepts and objects that were beyond his time. There are presumably people all over this diverse world who have similar visions of a future without war and pollution. I find it hard to find fault with the premise that money and fossil fuel extraction are culpable in this."

Don was really walking fast then, perhaps competing against something.

"Evolution has brought us to this point in time of scarcity, waste and environmental destruction. We live quite well. Money and fossil fuels helped us, no doubt. Money and fossil fuels powered us to the moon. Money and fossil fuels have provided great benefit to our species. But now it seems we need another revolution."

"I need a beer," Don said.

Our ideologies seemed at odds.

"Humans need to become the gods that they have conjured up in their minds for most of our history. But how? Is it possible yet? Have we as a species evolved to recognize ourselves as an integral part of one organism—the earth? Or are we the cancerous life form that is moving to smother and eliminate itself? These are the questions I grapple with."

"You g-grapple away; I'm gonna have a b-beer." He fished one out of his pack.

"The fact that the Venus project exists makes me optimistic. At least this is a vision of a way to live in harmony with each other and the great green and blue earth—an earth we are turning black."

"Mount Fuji's v-volcanic rocks were b-black b-before we came along."

I ignored him.

"Technology has to be the answer. The scientists and their scientific discoveries and inventions need to empower us to head off in new directions. The Internet is surely part of this revolution. The reality of our destructive systems needs to seep into the consciousness of more and more of our species. We need an education system that presents reality and lets kids experiment with it. An education system that fosters discovery over rote learning needs to gradually become standard. Innovation in all things surely has the power to carry us into a brighter future."

"We would need to c-create a new system," Don said. He gulped from his can as he powered up the mountain.

"We are innovating. It is happening all over. The Internet is powering acceleration in human achievement. We are conquering adversity in many new and exciting ways. But we are still powering our civilizations with oil."

"More oil!" he yelled. He held his arms aloft and danced a little jig.

"There are many who say the system we have is the only system that can work. They say that humans are merely animals with an internal drive to survive and enjoy life. A money-based economy allows for the largest benefit for the largest number. Sure, some get ridiculously rich while many suffer, but an increasing number of people live decent lives, and the lives of many are getting better. So what if our monetary system isn't based on anything other than debt? So what if the gap between rich and poor is widening? The homeland is protected. We are taking care of ourselves and those around us. Party on."

"Yeah! More ev-everything!"

"Overriding our human emotion seems insurmountable. I believe that our emotions will keep us fighting. Fairness can be legislated, but we circumvent at will."

"You are kind of d-depressing."

"My view is only one. There are over six billion others, and they will fight to make their views the *one*."

"Yep, w-we're doomed. G-get over it."

We fell silent for a while, just listening to the rhythmical sound of our boots on volcanic dirt.

"At least Jacques Fresco hints at a positive plan," I finally said.

* * *

The sun was coming up as we hiked the last few hundred metres, but we couldn't see it because there was a volcano in the way. We were hiking up the southern side, and the sun was rising, of course to the east. Fuji was blocking our way. We had to get to the top to see the view. I entered a trance. Using a walking stick I presume I had found, discarded by another hiker, I kept up a steady, strong pace. Don was behind me. We got to the summit as the sun was rising over Tokyo and the Pacific Ocean. Sticks with prayer flags were all over, fluttering in the wind. The noise of the flags sounded like clapping. We'd attained the roof of Japan to applause.

Don and I stood against the powerful wind. Clouds covered Tokyo. The Pacific Ocean stretched its blue to the horizon. We settled into quiet awe.

The top of Fuji-san is far from barren. There are buildings all over. Don and I spent hours skirting the edge of this ancient volcano. There were no people though, and nothing was open. Climbing season was over.

We walked around. There was a post office, and shops shuttered and silent. We nestled next to a building. Don fished a joint out of his jacket pocket. We smoked it in the peace of thin air.

"Did I tell you about the gambler I met while I was in Kuala Lumpur?" I asked.

"Nope. L-lay it on m-me."

"A couple of years ago I flew into Kuala Lumpur alone. Well, I was travelling alone. There were, of course, lots of other people flying into Kuala Lumpur that day."

Don's mouth crinkled into a smile.

"In fact, lots of people fly into Kuala Lumpur every day. It's a big city. The Petronas Towers were nearing completion."

"Petronas Towers?" he asked, eyebrows furrowed.

"Tallest office towers in the world. At least they were then."

Don's eyebrows relaxed.

"I got off the airport bus on a sunny, hot day deep in a city humming with activity in a peaceful, lazy way. I remember bright-coloured clothing and smiles. There was movement, but it wasn't hectic."

"Heat slows p-people down," he said.

"That's when I met her," I said expansively.

"Met w-who?"

"She wore stylish clothes and seemed sure of herself. She asked me where I was from. 'Canada,' I said. It seemed strange to me that she would be interested in a backpacking youth who had just got off a bus in a city square in Asia, so my guard was up."

Don puffed on the joint, the smoke captured by the wind.

"She invited me to sit on the low wall with her. Her sister, who was a nurse, was about to go to Canada to start work, and she wanted to talk. Guard still up, I sat down. Her English had just a hint of an accent. Minor grammar mishaps peppered her lilting delivery."

"Lilting d-delivery?" Don made a fist, his little finger raised like he was holding a teacup. Then he passed me the joint. I inhaled, feeling my mind expand. I passed it back and continued.

"I chatted with her for a few minutes. She talked about her sister's upcoming trip to Toronto. I talked about the fact that my sister is a nurse in Canada. My guard eased up as we spoke. She seemed genuine, but I was hot and sweaty. I wanted a shower and wanted to get rid of my backpack. I explained that I was grateful for the chat but that I was going to get going. She said that it would be great for me to meet her sister. Why didn't I come for a traditional Malaysian lunch with them? I said that if she really wanted that, then she should meet me in the square tomorrow morning. She agreed. I took my leave."

Don flicked the roach into the snow. "W-where d-did you go?"

"I found my hostel and refreshed myself. I met lots of other travelling youth. We all headed out to see what nightlife Kuala Lumpur had to offer."

"What d-did you do?" he asked.

"It involved loud music and bright lights," I replied.

"Sex, drugs and r-rock and r-roll," he added.

"The next morning, I went to the square, not expecting her to show up. However, there she was. I sat down again, curious. Could this be genuine? My guard was back up, but I was intrigued."

Don was smiling.

"We chatted for quite some time, and I grew to like this woman. She was engaging, and she laughed along with me as we talked about the world. I gradually became very comfortable with her. She mentioned that it was time to go back to her place and meet her sister, who would be off work soon. She said we would need to take a taxi and that, of course, since I was a guest, she would pay. On that sunny day I decided to make some new friends."

"So, you g-got in a taxi with a w-w-woman you'd just met in a ci-city you didn't know?" Don asked, a bit incredulous.

"Yep."

"Adventurous. K-keep t-talking," he said.

"During the cab ride, we talked about the upcoming takeover of Hong Kong by China. She spoke knowledgeably and earnestly. We arrived at a villa-type house in a pleasant neighbourhood. She paid the driver, and we went inside. It was open concept with leather couches and a big TV. A dining room table with chairs was on the other side of the couches in front of an opening to the kitchen. My companion quickly entered the kitchen and disappeared."

On one side of Fuji's summit was a huge antenna, maybe fifty feet high. I saw some guy wander out to it.

"Seated at one of the dining chairs was a man in his forties or fifties. He stood up with a big smile, extended his hand and introduced himself. We shook hands warmly and sat on the leather couches. He immediately explained that something had happened at the hospital and that the sister would be delayed. He asked me to stay for coffee and lunch, adding that the sister would be there soon. He told me that she was looking forward to meeting me."

"Where w-was the woman f-from the square?" Don asked.

"Gone," I replied. "In the kitchen somewhere."

"What was the m-m-man like?" Don asked, sitting up straighter.

"He was friendly and talked about the time he worked in the casinos in Niagara Falls. He talked about working at a casino now, in a hotel in Kuala Lumpur. In fact, he had been a dealer in casinos all his working life."

"He w-was a gambler f-for sure," Don said.

"Yep. A woman I had not seen before came out carrying a tray with a jar of instant coffee, some powdered milk and a bowl of sugar. There was also a mug of steaming water. I was to make my own coffee. I thought this was odd, but I didn't want to be rude, so I took a spoonful of each powder and made myself a drink. The man and I continued chatting as I sipped my instant coffee."

"Instant c-coffee is okay," Don said.

"I was alone with the man now, but the front door was open and I was the closest to it. Feelings of potential danger returned, but I was not particularly fearful. The man was originally from India. We drifted into a conversation about cricket."

"Ha! You used to tell me ab-about cricket a lot," Don said.

"I talked about watching test matches with my grandfather back in England. He talked about playing in the intense heat of his childhood home in India."

"Cricket is sl-slow, so slow. Nice to p-play in the heat," Don said.

"He loudly announced that it was time for lunch. We moved to the dining table, and I was offered more coffee. I declined. Lunch was delivered by another woman, who appeared from the kitchen, but aside from my cricket-loving companion, I rarely saw anyone else. The woman whom I'd met in the square had been gone since we arrived."

"Just y-you and the m-man," Don stated.

"Lunch was very pleasant—fish, vegetables and rice. We talked about all kinds of things, and I enjoyed the back and forth with this guy. The conversation eventually returned to gambling. He talked again about how he had been in the business for a long time. He talked about the casino he worked in now and said that if I was willing to go upstairs, he could teach me a trick or two that would guarantee I would win. We could then split the winnings."

Don and I were settled atop Mount Fuji, atop the roof of Japan. The building we were leaning against blocked the wind.

"I said that no, I was not a gambler. He said that I didn't have to be a gambler, because in about an hour he could teach me all that I needed to know. I said that I had come to talk to the nurse about Canada and that I still wanted to do that."

The scent of the atmosphere at the top of Fuji-san cleansed us. George floated into view. I continued telling my story. Don continued listening.

"The man in the villa locked eyes with me. He said that he could make us both a lot of money. He needed a lot of money because he had three wives, one in Canada."

"He had th-three wives?" Don asked.

"That's what he said. And he went on to say that the one in Canada was about to have a child and that I could be its godfather."

"What?"

"I know, crazy. I commiserated as best I could and tried to assure him that I understood how difficult having three wives must be. I expressed my apologies that I couldn't help him. He seemed surprised that I didn't want to be his child's godfather. I told him that I didn't feel comfortable doing so."

"Totally w-weird," Don said.

"It was different," I said, smiling at the understatement.

"Did you g-go upstairs?" Don asked.

"No way, man!"

Sitting at the summit of a snowy Fuji, I could feel the heat of Kuala Lumpur.

"The reality of the whole situation became crystal clear. Had I been blind? Fear hit me hard. My body experienced a flush of heat. The hairs on my neck stood to attention. My thoughts went to the coffee. I was the only one who had spooned the powder into that mug and drank it. My plate of food was almost gone. That plate had been given to me. If they had wanted to drug me, it would have been easy. On the inside I instantly became on fire, intensity mixed with fear. On the outside I remained calm. I was the Canadian guy who'd come to talk to the nurse. That pretense became who I was. The door to the outside remained open. I promised myself that at the first inkling of drugs in my system, I was out the door yelling."

Don's back was straight. The wind was quiet. "Then w-what did the dude s-say?" he asked.

"He said that the system was quite straightforward and that we would both make some easy money. He said that he needed me because the casino didn't know me."

"Whoa, w-w-weird. Intense."

"I thanked the gambler for what sounded like a great offer. I faked genuine interest. I then explained that I had come to talk to the sister about Canada and asked if she was coming."

Don unfolded his arms and rested his elbows on his knees.

"The gambler became quite persistent, trying his best to persuade me to help him, and help me, make money. All I had to do was follow him upstairs. However, I was steadfast. I was the Canadian guy there to give the nurse information about Canada."

"Why d-did he w-want you to go upstairs?"

"He said that all the gambling stuff was there and he could show me what to do. I told him that I wasn't a gambler, that I had come to talk to the nurse."

A cloud blocked the sun, and the wind rustled the snow.

"My original companion appeared. I turned to her and explained that really, I'd be happy to help her sister. I asked if she was coming."

Don had folded arms with his hood pulled tight.

"The man's phone rang then. He got up and walked to the door as he answered it and started talking. My exit was now blocked, but I had no sensation of narcotics in my system. I remained outwardly calm and relaxed. Inwardly, I felt hyper-alert and fully present. He was speaking loudly, giving the impression that the nurse was on the other end. He spoke about how I was there but that I would be disappointed that she couldn't come."

The top of Fuji was speckled with grey rocks protruding from white snow.

"He returned after the phone call to apologize that the nurse was unable to leave work and come. Maintaining the pretense that had brought all of us together that day, I expressed disappointment too. I said that I would be happy to meet her tomorrow."

The sun blazed again, and the wind died. Don and I sat warmly in the cold.

"My original companion would take me back downtown. The fear began to drain away as we said our goodbyes and left. Walking down the driveway, I realized I'd left my belt pouch with my camera. I had to go back. I ran inside and grabbed it."

"You w-went back?" Don asked.

"I had to get my camera, man! The gambler was still in the living room. I explained that I had left my belt pouch with my camera. He asked me to check to make sure it was still there. I said that I could feel it and that everything was okay."

"He demanded that I open the bag and make sure that it was there.

"I became worried. What was in there? I opened the pouch, took out my camera and showed it to him. He looked at me and said that he wanted to make sure that I knew that they hadn't taken anything."

Don let out a sigh.

"The gambler met my gaze; he was expressionless. I returned his stare. We stood like that for a few seconds. We would never see each other again, but we had spent hours chatting about cricket, gambling, families and many other things, all on a pretense. We were two men who had squared off and played a game of lies. I felt victorious."

"You w-were still alive." Don said. He looked at me with a bit of contempt.

"Then the man turned and went into the kitchen. I stood motionless for a few seconds, and then I surveyed the room. I returned to the sunshine and my original companion. We didn't talk much on the bus ride back. I paid. She made sure I got back to the square. We agreed to meet the next day. She would be with her sister. We both maintained the pretense."

Don unfolded his arms and peeled back his hood.

"My curiosity and my desire for closure remained. So, the next day I showed up at the arranged time. Of course, she wasn't there."

"Everybody l-lies," Don said.

After a bit of silence, I said, "I've thought about that episode since. I've always wondered if I could have made five thousand dollars in Kuala Lumpur."

Mostly I remembered the fear I felt, the sudden realization that I was alone with no idea where I was and with nothing but myself to rely on. Everyone was playing a part, like in a play or a scene from a movie. All my money was on me. It would have been so easy to drug me with that coffee. For all I know, they may have tried.

"Out of interest," I told him, "I googled 'gambling scam Kuala Lumpur' and found that in Vietnam, Thailand, Malaysia and other places people had had similar experiences. The stories were eerily similar in that victims were lured in with a story of a nurse heading to the victim's home country. While waiting, the marks were offered to be taught an easy gambling trick; they were lightly drugged so as to be more easily persuaded. Perhaps I too was drugged. But the sudden fear and sudden rush of adrenaline was maybe enough to help me plow through the narcotic and remain alert. I'll never know. But my memory of that day is clear. I look back on it fondly."

"You're l-lucky, my friend," Don said. He started walking. Me too.

* * *

We circled the summit, wandering the inner and outer edges of the peak. The wind battered our ears, so we rarely spoke. Mountains stretched into the distance, grey peaks with patches of white. Clouds blanketed Tokyo to the east; the sky was clear to the west. The sun's rays warmed us as we made our steady way around the caldera. We accepted the vistas as they appeared. Then we suddenly focused on something that wasn't the rectangular green rice paddies and winding grey roads below us. Our bodies stopped as our beings registered the shape. Fuji-san, Japan's volcano, presented itself in a full, perfect shadow stretching miles wide across the fields.

The sight of the mountain's shadow burned sharply into me.

* * *

Don and I walked side by side, descending, with the peak of Fuji receding. Don's arms swung more loosely, less stiffly and less tethered than before.

"So, what does reality mean?" I asked.

"What d-does it m-mean to you?" he replied, sending the question back at me.

"Well, it seems to me that there is a different reality for each human on this little planet. My perception of something is different from yours.

Trouble arises when I feel that my perception of what's real should also be your perception. If it isn't, I judge. I know I shouldn't, but I do. I can't seem to help myself."

We were walking fast, gravity lending us its power. Don's words glided my way. "Maybe you sh-should be a j-judge," he said.

"No way, amigo. Being a judge takes intense training."

"You c-can t-train yourself to be anything."

I glanced at him. We laughed. He continued.

"Okay, if th-there is no r-reality, then our l-lives don't really m-matter, so who c-cares, right? Just g-get on with it. Experience what l-l-life has to offer, r-really experience it, and try not to, l-like, care too much."

"But I care about almost all the things I experience. I emotionally care about a lot. Things slide my way, and I impose judgment upon them."

"Does that h-help?" he asked.

"Not at all, but I stack these judgments into my being and create a self. I act based on my judgments, and then I judge myself. It's wasteful, I know, but on and on I go, experiencing, judging and remonstrating."

"Why?" he wondered.

"Perhaps this is what life is? There is no reality really, just a bunch of perceptions jostling in a huge pool. Sometimes perceptions glom together with other, like perceptions and a force is generated. Soon different perceptions band together to vanquish other perception groups."

"You are sp-spiralling, man," he said.

"What do you think?" I asked.

"Well, b-buddy, in my m-mind, r-right now, like you said, reality is d-different for all of us. Reality d-doesn't, like, exist, just b-belief s-systems about reality. We h-have discovered that th-the earth is spherical. This is r-real. These k-kinds of reality are real. The earth is a sphere. Is my p-perception of the sphere the s-same as yours? Does it m-matter? The *earth is a sph-sphere*. The evidence is c-clear. So, I believe it," he said.

We were walking down switchbacks, back and forth like our words.

"Reality both exists and doesn't exist. I guess it is just a matter of scale. Some things are clearly real. Some things enter a grey area, and some things are essentially unknown or unknowable, like the future."

Don walked faster.

"As we age," I went on, "it seems that more and more of reality is becoming known. More and more things are becoming real. We as a species, and we as life on earth, are becoming aware of more and more. Reality becomes a bigger and bigger part of us."

He turned to me and grinned. "More e-everything!" he said.

* * *

"You moved away from the canal a few years back, right?" I asked.

"You betcha," Don said.

"When you did live near it, did you walk along it much?"

"I r-ran along it. I w-was training for a m-marathon."

We were talking about the Rideau Canal in Ottawa, a stretch of water created by human toil well over a hundred years ago, the setting for pleasure boats during the summer and ice skating in the winter.

Don looked down the length of the trail, "There's n-nobody here. We are al-alone," he said.

I got to thinking about canals. People found that moving themselves and their things around in boats made great sense. The water took the weight, and for many of us it was all around. Big ships started to ply the waterways of the world, discovering new lands and carrying goods for trade. A couple of places, Panama and Suez, were narrow bits of land that required long journeys to navigate around.

Don's jacket was tied around his waist. We continued descending.

"What was your time for the marathon?" I asked.

"Not bad."

"Did you run with anybody?"

"Nope." His replies were blunt. I kept fishing.

"How many months did you train?"

"F-five."

"Did you train with anybody?"

"No."

"Did you wear elephant ears for the race?"

"Shut u-up!"

We continued in silence, but I was smiling and the air was warming.

People have been building canals for many centuries all around the world. These days, the technology involved is amazing. Waterworks carry massive ships up and up and then down and down to get across land formations.

The canal system that joins Ottawa to Kingston is the oldest in North America. It was built for military reasons in the early 18th century to ensure there was a way from Montreal to Kingston without having to go close to the USA via the St. Lawrence, but it was also important for trade. The canal runs through Ottawa, but the entire Rideau Waterway involves a series of locks that join lake to river to lake, covering 200 kilometres.

Ottawa is a cold winter city; the canal freezes for a few months. Somewhere along the way they started clearing the snow and flooding its length. The ice created is pretty good for skating—and Canada has many skaters. The canal gets crowded on the weekend days when the weather cooperates. Just below the freezing point is best. Too warm and they shut it down. Too cold and most skaters can't be bothered.

Ottawa has a winter festival every year called Winterlude. The canal hosts many events. Ice sculptures are carved, and skillful artisans demonstrate their prowess.

The canal winds its way pleasantly through Ottawa. Paths flank its sides; boats ply its length in summer; people don skates and speed down its length in the winter. The drive along it is a favourite of visiting guests. No longer used for trade or business, it has become a tourist attraction.

Later, Don and I were high-fiving and backslapping by the car in the parking lot of Fuji.

"Right on, man, we did it! Five mountains in six days."

"R-right on!"

* * *

We got in the car. There was no sign of the green and white VW van. We descended toward fields and towns, the road from Fuji winding through woods.

"Somewhere near here is the suicide forest," I said.

Why had I chosen to mention that? Why was I so depressing?

"It's called Aokigahara. Last year, a record number chose this forest as their final resting place."

Don stared out the window. The trees flew by. He sipped his beer.

"Why g-go all the way to the f-forest?" he asked. "I w-would just ingest p-potent p-pills on my couch. I love my c-couch. Black leather."

"Good point," I offered.

Soon we were driving between buildings and through traffic lights. Don's chiselled, close-cropped head saw the electric mayhem of ordered chaos. Some houses looked like postcards with their gleaming peaked rooves and immaculate gardens encircled by walls, the trees and bushes sculpted, the gardens weed-free, the stone pagodas radiating stoicism. Next to these nice dwellings were overgrown lots with dirty puddles and rusted appliances. Stained wooden houses squatted nearby. Overhead cables criss-crossed it all.

Don turned to me. "I'm sad," he said. "No more m-mountains."

"Don't worry," I said. "We've got a night in Tokyo. There'll be stairs to climb."

Grey pollution haze shrouded the big city and shaded the sky. I steered the car next to a booth, and we took our ticket. We spent the next two hours on the highway, watching the density of the city stack around us.

"Are you gonna call Jean as soon as you get back?" I asked.

"Yes."

"Are you gonna start work as soon as you get back?"

"Definitely. There'll be p-plenty of c-coding to do."

The highway curved by buildings that were taller and taller, closer and closer to the edge of the road. Sometimes the highway was seven stories high, making our heads level with office windows. We could see the rows of desks and the tracks of fluorescent lights brightening the clean spaces, the dirt under our fingernails contrasting with sterility as we sped by.

"I drove into Tokyo a couple of times when I was driving," I mentioned.

"During th-the Olympics?" Don asked.

"Yeah. I drove a van. I scooped up people who had flown into Narita and then whisked them up to Nagano."

"Anyone in-interesting?"

"I drove this rich lady and her husband. He didn't say much, but she didn't stop talking. Told me about life in Portland."

Don adopted a posh British accent. "Oregon, I presume?"

I did the same. "Yes, the Northwest. By the ocean, don't you know."

The traffic was getting thick. I had to pay attention as I talked.

"She owned horses," I said. "Lots and lots of horses. She talked non-stop about horses. I politely nodded and tried to listen."

"She s-saddled you with stories."

We looked at each other and smirked.

"She told me that a cross between a zebra and a donkey is called a zonkey."

"*Zoinks!*" he yelled in a great Scooby-Doo impression.

CHAPTER 8

Tokyo

The traffic ahead ground to a halt. We spent the next hour creeping into Tokyo. Finally, we exited, paid our toll and then negotiated the traffic lights of the city. I'd arranged a parking space behind Yoshiko's building.

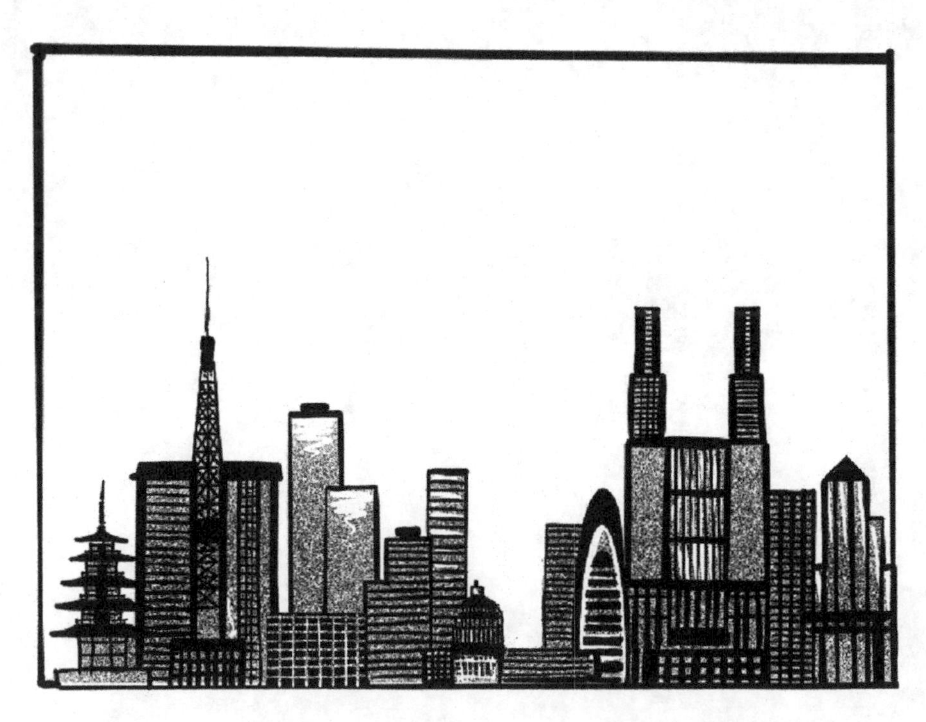

I found a grey phone at the side of Ogikubo station, next to the road. I stopped. We got out of the car. I inserted my card, then I pressed the buttons. The phone rang. Yoshiko answered. I sensed her bright smile.

"Moshi moshi," she said.

"Hey, how ya doing?" I asked.

"Genki desu yo." She was well.

"We're here. Where do you want to meet Kate?" I asked.

"Harajuku station, west exit."

"Great. What time?"

"Seven," she said.

"I'll call Kate," I said.

Kate now lived in Tokyo, writing the odd article for the *Japan Times.* I called her.

"Moshi moshi. Gary?" she asked.

"Yeah. How's it going, Kate?"

"Crazy, as usual," she said.

"Can you meet us at Harajuku station at seven?"

"Yeah. What exit?"

"West."

"See you then."

Don watched me hang up the phone. "How d-do you kn-know Yoshiko?" he asked.

"I met her a few years ago in Tokyo," I said.

"When you were t-teaching th-there?" he asked.

"Yep," I answered. "I used to work for an agency that supplied English teachers to companies and schools. I used to take trains every day."

His body seemed energized. "So, was Yoshiko a student?" he wondered.

I think he knew the answer. I tried to talk. "Yes, but ..." I was aware of the negative reaction this admission might elicit.

He cut me off immediately. "You d-dog!"

* * *

The memory of meeting Yoshiko was fresh despite the intervening years. I sat in a room high up in a Tokyo building. I'd already taught two young men one-on-one English lessons. It was usual first-lesson stuff, gauging their English-language ability, determining their interests and working together to chart a course.

The last student of the day was a young woman. When she entered the room, I was immediately taken with her smile.

Her English was the best I'd encountered in my years teaching in Japan, easily the most natural. As the initial chat moved to life stories, I found that she'd spent three years during high school studying in an American academy in Switzerland. I smiled at her smile and felt myself attracted to her, our conversation occasionally entering the realm of subtle flirting.

Outside the window, the buildings of the Tokyo government could be seen below. The buildings were regal, strong and impressive without being ostentatious. We began to talk about what was out the window, the seat of power in Japan. I asked questions, and she answered. I felt that my job was to ask questions, to encourage the use of English, to keep her talking, to keep her practicing. Eventually we were standing, getting ready to leave. She moved toward the window and leaned over the recessed ledge. I had a view of the Tokyo cityscape in the distance and of an attractive woman in the foreground.

* * *

Don and I got back in the car. We drove and parked, then took the elevator up to Yoshiko's apartment. We were deep in the density of Tokyo, where the roads were paved, the houses were small and the air was city-like.

"Hi, Honey!" I said when she let us in. We hugged and kissed.

"Hi, Yoshiko," Don said. His bulky form filled the doorway.

"Let's go," she said.

We entered the elevator. "How was it?" She was looking at Don.

"Awesome," he said. "Fuji was sp-spectacular." The doors opened on the main floor.

We walked through a warren of houses, neatly arranged along the edges of narrow roads. We breathed in the autumn air and adopted the brisk pace of youth.

"Where are we going?" I asked.

"I found a famous restaurant in Harajuku." Yoshiko's brilliance was dazzling, as usual. "It's famous for yakitori," she added.

"Hara-where, yaki-w-what?" Don laughed.

"Harajuku is in Tokyo. There are lots of young people there. Yakitori is roast chicken on a stick. You dip them in sauces," Yoshiko said. She was holding my hand.

"Nice." Don said.

We entered a covered shopping street. Lofty ceilings with windows protected the stores from weather. Colourful plastic merchandise, practically arranged, was pushed onto the street. Don surveyed the chaotic order.

He had spotted the liquor store and its adjacent vending machine. "Beer?" he enquired.

"Certainly, sir," I replied.

"Yoshiko?" he asked.

"No thanks," she said.

Coins found their way into the machine; buttons were pushed. After a *clunk-clunk*, two cans of Kirin lager appeared. He handed one to me.

We entered Asagaya station, Yoshiko bought three tickets, and we filed through turnstiles and walked up the stairs. On the platform, Don asked, "Why is it so c-clean?"

Yoshiko shrugged. The train arrived. Don and I sipped our beers as we stepped through the open doors.

* * *

We met Kate on the platform when she arrived on her connecting train. Yoshiko led the way. Kate walked with her. Don and I followed.

We walked off the street and through a door into a restaurant. There was a low buzz of conversation and a haze of cigarette smoke. We were led to a shiny table.

Tokyo abounds with eating establishments. The Japanese take their food and its taste very seriously. Owing to the sheer size and population of Tokyo, there are restaurants everywhere.

We'd entered an *izakaya*, a drinking/eating establishment where a group of people gather and order a bunch of food and a bunch of drinks. At the end of the session, the bill is divided by the number of people there. What individual people ate or drank doesn't matter; the bill is divided evenly, no question, no arguments, no tension. We are all one.

After we sat down, Kate said, "So, did you have a good time? Where did you go?"

I answered, "We had an epic road trip."

Kate waited. I glanced at Don. He seemed happy. I elaborated, saying, "We drove from Sendai to Bandai-san, then we hiked some mountains in Nagano. We just drove here from Fuji-san."

"Did you camp?" she asked.

"Oh yeah," Don said. Kate looked at Don. Don looked at Kate.

Yoshiko flagged down a waiter, saying, "Sumimasen!" We all ordered drinks and started to look at the menu. There were pictures of steaming bowls, breaded delicacies on plates, salads, and fish staring at us with mysterious eyes.

Yoshiko asked us what we wanted to eat. "Fish." Don said in a jovial way. Yoshiko ordered a bunch of food.

The place had floor-to-ceiling windows that bounced our camera flashes back at us. Plates of food arrived, and chopsticks clacked morsels into our mouths. Our glasses remained full.

Yoshiko sipped a blue drink. She asked Kate, "How's work? You write for the *Japan Times*, right?"

"I'm an editor, but I write the occasional article. My boss wants me to work faster."

A waiter dropped by and asked if we needed anything.

Kate said, "Hai, mo hitosu kudasai" (Yes, another one please).

Yoshiko said, "Watashi mo" (Me too).

I ordered beers for Don and me. The waiter carefully placed our empty glasses on a tray. He walked away, fully engaged in the task at hand.

Yoshiko mentioned that she was leaving for Spain soon.

Kate said, "Yeah, Gary was saying. You're gonna study Spanish, right? Where?"

"Salamanca."

"Where's that?"

"Near Portugal."

"Why learn Spanish?"

"I love Spanish!"

"Great reason!"

We laughed. The waiter came by with our drinks. Kate played with the umbrella in hers. Yoshiko sipped from her straw. Don sipped. I didn't touch mine.

Kate said, "Tell me how you met Gary. He told me. Now I'm ready to hear the real story."

We all laughed.

"Well, he taught me for three months."

"He said your English was amazing, that he had nothing to teach you."

Yoshiko giggled into her hand. She looked directly at Kate. "Back then I had a boyfriend and Gary had a girlfriend. But we definitely liked each other."

"He liked you, that's for sure," Kate said.

"Right after the last lesson, we took a day trip to Izu Peninsula, in Shizuoka Prefecture. We hitchhiked to a small beach and back to a train station. This was my first hitchhiking experience. I had lots of fun."

"He never told me that! Izu?"

We all laughed.

"We stayed in touch for three years. Normally he called me up every couple of months, and I took him to hip restaurants in Tokyo for lunch or dinner."

"And now why are you guys together?"

"Gary's parents visited Japan early this summer. I took them out for lunch in Shibuya. The restaurant name is Setsugekka."

"What does that mean?"

"Snow … moon … flower?" Yoshiko said. It took her awhile to translate.

"The Restaurant of the Snow Moon Flower. Was it nice?"

"It had a pleasantly modern but definitely Japanese atmosphere. We needed to sit on the floor, which was the only regrettable thing because Gary's parents looked uncomfortable."

"When my parents came, they didn't like sitting on the floor," Kate said.

"It's so good for you!"

Kate nodded vigorously.

"Sendai is only two hours by bullet train from Tokyo. He invited me to his place. I'd already quit my job, and furthermore I'd never been to Sendai before, so I visited him. He took me to Yama-dera."

"I've been there, up a cliff."

"He took me camping near Bandai-san and to the beautiful coast near Matsushima. It was the end of summer. It was during that trip that we decided on seeing each other even though we knew I was going to Spain."

Kate smiled. Her chin rested on her hand.

***

George was only a memory. He'd been dead for over ten years, but sometimes he drifted into my mind.

Don, George and I were wild that night. We were frenzied teenagers in someone else's backyard. I remember a swimming pool. How did we get there? Don and George started throwing lawn furniture into the water. I watched. I didn't stop them.

***

The next day, Don and I took a Narita Express to the airport. We didn't order beers.

CHAPTER 9

The Departure of Don Philips

Don flew to Japan to see me. I flew to Japan to lose myself, to lose a Western experience and gain an Eastern one. I hoped that Don could lose the need to drink alcohol.

"So, you're an alcoholic?" I asked. Don nodded. I put my arm around his broad shoulders and, with compassion, asked, "What does that mean?"

The train moved quietly, all clean and vacuumed. He looked at me. "Why am I s-so ang-angry?" he asked, avoiding my question with one of his own.

"You've always been angry. That's part of the reason I enjoy being with you," I said. I realized that I was angry too. I suppressed my anger, though. *Is that why I have MS?* Don looked down, his hand on his forehead.

I didn't know what to say, so I tried, "I love talking to you, man. Thanks for coming." The landscape continued presenting its blurry views through the train window.

Soon enough we stopped at Terminal 2. The announcement blasted this banality. We made our way up escalators and down hallways. His visit was over. We had hiked up and down five mountains, we had caught up, and he had experienced the efficient energy of Japan.

"Let's have some *kaiten* sushi," I said.

"Sounds g-good," he agreed. We sat on stools and watched little plates trundle by. I scooped green tea into a cup and pressed it into the hot water dispenser. So did Don.

"I'm gonna s-stop d-drinking for a while," he said.

"Sounds good."

We looked out the big windows at aircraft taking off and landing. We saw humanity flexing its technological muscles. Don used one big hand to grab a small plate of shrimp sushi; he used the other to sip hot tea.

An image of George flickered behind Don's big body. I tried to hold on to the present moment, but as always, it vanished after it appeared.

I suddenly asked, "Why do you think George killed himself?" It was blunt. I didn't know how to ask such a question.

"He went off his medication," Don said, shrimp sushi entering his mouth. He paused while he chewed, watching a plane through the window. "George s-said that he didn't f-feel himself while he was on it."

"Sad," I stated.

"Yeah," he said, reaching for more sushi, deep red tuna. His pile of empty plates grew faster than mine. More everything.

We made our way to airport customs.

I said to Don, as he was getting ready to leave, "Channel that anger, man. It's powerful stuff."

He looked at me. His eyes were glistening. We shook hands, patted each other's backs and remained silent throughout. Then he turned and wandered through customs, placed his things on a conveyer belt and walked through a metal detector. Then he disappeared around a corner. George too.

I watched people shuffling in queues, wheeling cases, dealing with their own beliefs.

EPILOGUE

Two Years After Our Mountain Adventure in Japan

Yoshiko and I got married in Canada. Don was standing next to the centre aisle as we walked by. He looked me in the eye and said, "Best wedding ever, man."

I'll always remember the look in his eyes when he was connected to the moment.

Five Years After Our Mountain Adventure in Japan

Don Philips flew to the Philippines today. He left his wife, Jean, his job, his house, his mortgage, his cubicle, his country. He left it all—dropped it like a hot potato plucked from the fire—and leapt into freedom, leaving in his wake all the trappings of his mind. I'm sure when he arrived, he realized that he'd taken his mind with him, the dark stormy clouds still raging through his head, whipping up a frenzy of self-doubt, rage and angst. But there is no conflict there, no one to hurt. At least he's not witnessing first-hand the emotional pain he inflicts on others. Now, for him, the wound of his absence is distant. After he drinks a few more beers, it will be gone.

Seven Years After Our Mountain Adventure in Japan

I received a message from Don's mom a couple of days ago. Don passed away in the Philippines. He'd been living there for two years. Officially, he'd died of a heart attack. He was just about to turn 42.

Don, buddy, you had *everything* going for you—good looks, charisma, integrity, intelligence and superior athletic ability. How could alcohol conquer you?

At the funeral, his sister said, "Now Don is with George."

Printed in the United States
By Bookmasters